BILL AND TY GET HIGH
RICKY FRY

an aerobic gypsy book

ISBN 978-0-9988813-0-0
Published April 20, 2017
United States of America

an aerobic gypsy book

For all of my crazy friends—
past, present, and future.

1.

Ty was 19 years old when he took his first hit of marijuana—late to the game by stoner standards. It was college, a time of experimentation and discovery, and the girl holding the bong was hot. He was sprawled on the floor, staring up at a Kid Cudi poster, when he knew he didn't want to be a lawyer.

"Mom. Dad. I'm dropping pre-law," he said. "I'm going to become an art major."

After one semester of failed classes he dropped out altogether. "I need to find myself. Art can't be rushed."

So he moved into a tiny apartment in Capitol Hill with his best friend Bill.

Now they sit together on a ratty couch, Ty shirtless and Bill wearing a velvet smoking jacket. They work silently, scraping mossy flakes of resin from glass pipes. The lighter clicks. Suck and puff. Pass. Repeat. Now they're high.

Ty sinks deep into the cushions and looks up at the ceiling. He thinks about his ex. "Bill?"

"Yeah?" Bill is thinking about where they're gonna get more weed.

"Do you think Tiffany broke up with me because my feet smell so bad?" He looks down at his skinny toes.

"Aw, don't say that. She broke up with you because she's a bitch."

"Hey, man. She's not a bitch."

"Alright, she's not a bitch. She's a whore."

"Dude!"

"Okay, okay. She broke up with you because she never appreciated your potential. She's narrow minded, man." He smiles. "You're awesome, bro."

"Aw, thanks." Ty's face turns red and he looks away. "I just miss her sometimes."

"I know, man. I know." Bill stares off into the empty space of the room for a minute, slaps his knee. "We need music!" He grabs a remote from the water-stained coffee table and soon a beat streams through a pair of speakers. Bill sings and Ty plays air drums until they're both out of breath.

Ty laughs. "Wanna smoke again?"

"Dude, we just smoked the last bit of resin."

"Damn. What about the grinder? There's gotta be some keef."

"We scraped it clean, remember? Smoked the keef last night." A fly buzzes near Bill's head. He swats and misses. "We're dry as Mormons, little Ty."

Ty pretends to cry. "Why don't we call Kenny? He's always got weed."

"Kenny's out of town, man. Went up to the mountains for some kind of romantic weekend with his girl."

"She's such a downer."

"Don't worry," says Bill. "We know more than one stoner."

Bill goes to shower. When Ty hears the water running he drops his shorts to his ankles and masturbates. He's thinking of bong girl, the one from college, when he cums on his skinny belly and cleans up with a greasy paper towel left over from last night's pizza. He's disposing of the evidence when Bill returns from the shower, still wearing the smoking jacket.

"Dude, you're obsessed with that stupid thing."

"Did I just hear you masturbating?"

"Um—"

"Never mind. I've got an idea."

2.

They stare up at Pedro's third-floor apartment from the street. Hip hop pours through the open balcony door. Bill picks a small rock from the ground and takes aim at the open doorway. He misses and the rock hits glass.

Pedro rushes onto the balcony, a cloud of smoke behind him. He wears nothing but a pair of tighty whities, his pudgy belly hanging over the elastic waistband. "What are you idiots doing? You'll break the fucking glass."

"Hey, Pedro!" Ty smiles and waves back. "Buzz us in, bro."

An old lady shouts from an opposite balcony. "I warned you!" She points a rolled up newspaper like a weapon. "First those damn marijuana cigarettes and your filthy gangster rap—now it's shouting and throwing rocks. The manager will hear about this!"

"Aw, Mrs. Jensen." Pedro smiles and opens his palms toward her in the Jesus pose—a chubby little Mexican angel. "Don't tell the manager. He might evict me, and you'll miss me when I'm gone."

She mumbles and lights a Parliament. Pedro disappears into the apartment and soon Bill and Ty hear the buzzer. They ride a slow elevator to the third floor and follow the smell of herb to Pedro's door.

He opens it before they can knock. "Crazy fucking gringos, why don't you text first like normal people?"

"Didn't pay the phone bill." Bill points back over his shoulder. "Your neighbor seems pretty upset."

"Don't mind the old bitch." Pedro walks over to the open balcony and leans his head out. "She's just mad because SHE'S NOT GET-TING LAID!"

Ty winces. "Dude, that's fucked up."

"What? She likes it when I talk dirty to her." He laughs and pulls up the sagging rear of his underwear. "Let me guess. You fools want me to smoke you up?"

Ty looks hurt. "Come on, Pedro. It's not like that. We came by to see you—to see what you're painting."

"Ah, I'm fucking with you fools. Get in here! Let's blaze one." They sit on a wide leather couch and Pedro opens a wooden box on a lami-nated Swedish coffee table.

In another minute they're smoking. They pass the bowl until it's cashed and then Pedro packs another. The apartment fills with sweet haze while Slacker plays tracks by Snoop, Wiz Khalifa, Atmosphere, and Method Man. They melt into the couch, smiling.

In the dining area, where a table might normally be, is an easel. A stretched canvas is covered in bright shades of blue and white and darker shades of gray. It's a man; the head is a giant triangle. He smokes a triangular joint and melts upward into the night sky.

"You like the painting?"

Ty says, "Yeah, man. I can't stop staring at it."

"I sold it." Pedro grinds another bowl and talks. "Snapped up for $350. Some lawyer up in Boulder, I guess. Good thing too, because the rent's due next week."

Bill groans. "Ugh. Don't remind us."

Pedro lights the bowl, takes a hit and passes it to Ty. "Oh shit, you guys hear what happened to Jackson?"

"Nah, man. We haven't seen that guy in a while." Ty draws a long hit and passes the pipe to Bill.

"That's because he's in jail."

"What?"

"Yeah. Got pulled over on Lincoln with some chick he met at the bar. He was drunk, and she was doing a line of coke on the dashboard."

"Fuck. Why didn't anyone call us?"

"We tried. You didn't pay the bill, remember?"

Bill shrugs.

Ty takes another hit. "Is there anything we can do?"

"Bail is five grand. So yeah, he's fucked."

"Five fucking grand?" Smoke pours from Ty's lips and he sinks back into the couch. "We can't even make rent."

"It's messed up." Pedro goes to work loading another bowl. "Hey Bill, how's that book you're writing—the one about the future where corporations get everyone hooked on drugs and build giant prisons?"

"I'm still working on it. But right now I'm working on a book about a couple of fuckups who kidnap a celebrity for ransom money."

"Right—" Pedro brings the pipe to his lips. Flick. "Man, I don't know why you want to write books." Inhale. Hold. Cough. "No one reads anymore, especially not stoners." Cough.

"I'm a stoner and I read all the time."

"That's because you're pretentious—you think you're better than everyone."

"That's not true."

"It's true," says Ty. He flips around on the couch and hangs his legs over the back. "Pedro, your painting looks awesome upside down."

"Thanks, little bro."

Bill pouts. "I am not pretentious."

"Then why are you wearing a velvet smoking jacket?" Pedro laughs his big Mexican laugh and grabs at his round belly. "You think you're some kind of character in a movie?"

"This is style." Bill smooths the velvet jacket with his open palms. "When's the last time you changed your underwear?"

"Don't be rude. Not after I smoked you up." Pedro laughs again. "Relax, man. You need another hit."

"Yeah," says Ty. "Take another hit."

They all take another hit, then another, and the beats keep playing. An hour passes. Ty falls asleep with his legs hanging over the couch and Bill imagines the big kidnap scene in his novel. Then Pedro gets a text and says they have to go.

"Shit!" Ty rubs his thighs. "My fucking legs fell asleep." He tries to stand and falls back on the couch. "It hurts!"

Pedro is unsympathetic. "Don't overstay the homie welcome. I've got shit to do."

He's still in his underwear when he closes the door behind them.

3.

Joe Campbell first went to juvenile detention at the age of fifteen for beating a schoolmate senseless in a fit of rage. Six months out of lockup he shot another teenager in the back of the leg in retaliation for the beating of his younger brother—walked right up behind him in the front yard and pulled the trigger.

But it was assaulting a police officer that sent him back to juvie and then on to county jail, where two inmates made a grab for him in the shower. It took eight deputies in full riot gear to drag him naked and hysterical to an isolation cell.

After months in solitary confinement, interrupted only by sessions of psychological testing, he was transferred—under heavy sedation—to a state mental health facility. The diagnosis was paranoid schizophrenia. A young doctor took an experimental interest in him and prescribed varying medications and dosages. Sometimes it got worse, or Joe couldn't think at all. Days passed without memory. But other times the voices lessened, or he went a day without any visions. It continued like this—the young doctor fine-tuning—until the ideal combination of drugs and therapy was reached, and he could think clearly again.

A year later he was released. But no one would hire him, so he lived on the streets. He skipped his medications. He did drugs. He ended up in San Francisco. Then one day, when it was cold and gray and he was hungry, a man handed him a hundred dollars and a bus ticket to

Colorado. So he bought a hot sandwich from a friendly Vietnamese family—they had a little cart outside the station—and got on the bus.

Now he's in Denver. Fucking Denver. Where the winters are cold and the summers are hot like a desert. Where the cops will ticket you for sleeping under a tree in the park so you freeze at night in the alleyway. Or crawl into a dumpster. So he sells drugs and buys a coffee from McDonald's and sits inside where it's warm until the manager tells him to buy something else or get out.

But today it's hot. Too hot for Joe. He sweats on the corner of Colfax and Pennsylvania, waiting for people to buy his pills. Then he sees these two skinny hipsters, walking and talking. They probably like pills.

"Hey man," he says to the one in the tank top, "you want some pills?"

But the skinny hipster shakes his head and says no, we don't do that stuff.

"I've got Percocet," says Joe.

But the grinning idiot shakes his head again and says no thanks.

"Then what do you want? A little tar?" Goddamn, he thinks, I must be the most helpful drug dealer in America.

But these hipsters just keep saying, "We're good. We're good." And he thinks, if you were good, you'd buy my drugs.

He's thirsty and hungry and he needs to buy something so he can just use the bathroom in the 7/11 so finally he says to them, "Man, just give me a fucking dollar!"

Then the second hipster, the one wearing that stupid jacket on a hot day, waves his arms around and shouts, "Fuck you, asshole!"

Joe feels the blood stirring in his arteries. His vision dims. And he cracks his neck, pop pop pop, the way he always does before he delivers a beating.

Tires screech. A black minivan comes to a hard stop along the sidewalk and the skinny hipsters climb in, speed away.

And Joe is left alone on the corner, shaking his head, trying to decide if what he just saw was real.

4.

The driver of the black minivan turns to Bill, riding shotgun. "Who the fuck was that?"

"Just some bum."

"You're lucky I was passing by. He could have killed you."

"I told him to fuck off." Bill laughs. "Don't worry, Brian. I can handle myself."

Brian looks at the velvet jacket and chuckles. "Are you serious? Anyway, what are you two assholes doing? Besides getting into trouble with the locals?"

Ty speaks up in his cheerful tone, "We came from Pedro's place."

Bill says, "We're out of weed."

"It's your lucky day, 'cause I've got some weed back at the crib. I'll smoke you up."

"Damn, Brian. That's the shit, bro."

"Just gotta pick up lunch. You idiots know the Bourbon Grill over on Gilpin?"

"It's dank," says Ty. He rubs at his belly.

"Best chicken in Denver."

Brian orders a combination meal with rice, chicken, mac and cheese, fries, and a soda. Bill and Ty comb their pockets for a few dollars and split a large order of salty french fries. They wait outside the tiny storefront, nothing more than a walk up window with a red awning, and watch the traffic on Colfax. An ambulance roars past, siren wailing, help is on the way. Two more people with sad faces ask for dollars, but Ty answers this time, "Sorry, we spent it all on fries." Bill grumbles. Then they're back in Brian's van, driving to his place out in Aurora. The apartment's a dump and rent is cheap, just the way he likes it.

They spread out on his big tan couch, watch a flat-screen TV, eat chicken and rice and french fries and pause to pass the pipe.

"Marijuana and deep fried potatoes." Bill shoves a fry into his mouth. "Maybe life is worth living after all."

Ty throws a greasy fry at Brian. "What's up with the suit, bro?"

"I'm working. You know, work, that thing most people do every day."

"Oh, yeah—work." Suck. Hold. Cough. "You still driving around dead people?"

"Making good money, and I got my benefits from the Army coming in."

Bill looks around the room. "Whatcha doing with all that money? Your place is a fucking dump."

"Saving. You idiots should try it. Gonna open my own business soon—Brian's Discount Dog Food."

"Dog food?" Bill laughs as he says it out loud.

"You think it's funny? Take a look around this city and all you see are dogs. And people love their fucking dogs, man."

"It's true," says Ty. "My mom spent seven grand on the dog's hip replacement."

Bill laughs. "You should see his parent's place. There's like a hundred pictures of the damn dog and not one of Ty."

Ty shakes his head. "Seven thousand dollars and the dog dies a few months later."

Brian laughs and loads another bowl. He starts a video game; there's the sound of virtual death, soldiers and aliens hacked down with explosions and gunfire.

Bill thinks it's a good time to ask. "Brian, you got any extra weed we could borrow?"

"How much you looking for?"

"An eighth, man. Something to last us a couple days."

"Wish I could help you out but my weed's gotta last until payday."

"Damn."

"Why don't you just call Kenny?"

"He's out of town, remember? The weekend thing with his girl?"

Brian rolls his eyes. "She's such a fucking downer, man."

Ty blows smoke through his nose. "That's what I'm always saying."

"Things haven't been the same since they moved in together. Remember the parties we used to have?"

"She put an end to that shit." Ty passes to Bill, swings his legs over the back of the couch and kicks his shoes off.

Brian pauses the game and sniffs the air. "What's that smell?"

"Ty's feet," says Bill. "They're chemical weapons."

"Damn, Ty. Put your shoes back on." He watches Ty shove his bare toes into a pair of torn, black Vans. "Don't you ever wear socks?"

Ty only laughs.

Bill shrugs his shoulders. "You get used to it."

A cell phone rings and Brian answers. Bill listens to him take the call, notices how professional he sounds, his voice changing into something deeper and much more serious, confident. When Brian hangs up he pulls a small plastic bottle from his suit pants, squeezes a tiny drop into each eye. "Come on, we've got a pickup."

"A pickup?"

"Yeah, and it's a rush job."

Ty wishes he hadn't smoked so much. "Like a real dead body? In the van? With us?"

"It's in a bodybag, dumbass." He grabs his keys from the coffee table, pulls his jacket straight and unwraps a fresh stick of gum. "Don't be such a bitch."

He steers the black minivan through narrow streets and alleys to bypass traffic. Bill rides shotgun and Ty sits on one of the empty gurneys secured side-by-side in the back. They pull into a hospital loading dock and Brian tells them not to do anything stupid. Then he disappears beneath the hospital.

When he makes his way back to the van there's the shape of a person on the gurney, covered by a shaggy, purple blanket. A pillow sticks out from beneath a lump where the head must be.

Bill reminds himself to breathe. "Holy shit. I think I'm gonna be sick."

"Not here." He rolls the gurney into the van with a giant push, throwing all of his weight behind it, grunting and digging in his heels. The van rocks on its suspension as the gurney slides into place. "Let's go."

They're pulling away from the hospital when Ty asks, "Who is it?"

"Some old lady, could be anyone's grandma."

"How'd she die?" Ty studies the shape beside him. Bill looks straight ahead.

"Old age I guess." Then he straightens up in the seat and says, "Look, I don't really know much about these people and I don't ask. They're just bodies in the back of my van."

"Death—" Bill brings his hand to his chin in academic posture. "I never thought about it before, but it must be quite the business."

"You have no idea." Brian glances at Ty in the rear-view mirror.

"Take this old lady for example. She's going to the organ donor people—the folks with the little red coolers."

"Are they gonna donate her heart?"

"No, no. Nothing like that. She's much too old to donate her heart,
heck, even her bones are no good. They're gonna strip her skin."

"Her skin?" Ty shudders.

"Yep. Strip it right down to the muscle."

"For what?"

"There's a corporation out on the East Coast somewhere, makes
an expensive surgical implant out of the stuff. Last time I checked
their stock was up."

Bill says, "Is that legal?"

"Sure—long as you've got that tiny heart on your driver's license
they can take whatever they want—and they do." He unwraps another
stick of gum and slides it between dingy teeth.

Ty imagines mad surgeons in a dark operating room, blood splat-
tered across their masks, pulling bodies apart with medieval hooks
and rusty saw blades.

Brian chews his gum and continues, "They're making money,
those guys cutting up bodies all day—the whole place is making
money. Hell, I'm making money driving the damn stiffs back and
forth. Everyone's making money except the family of the poor
chump who died." He's quiet for a moment, then he says, "Kinda
fucked up, really."

Bill says to pull over he has to throw up. Brian pulls the minivan
into a parking lot and Bill gets out to vomit. He's standing there, bent
over the asphalt, when the cop pulls up behind them.

Whoop! There's the quick squawk of a police siren, then the door
opening, the officer adjusting her gun belt, walking toward Brian in
the driver's seat while she tells Bill to stay put and show his hands. Ty
wonders if he'll see Jackson in jail.

"Driver's license," she says in a matter-of-fact police officer tone.
"Registration."

"I apologize, officer. He's carsick."

She stares at him in his grey suit, then cranes her neck to look in the back, sees Ty in his tank top and shorts riding next to the body-bag and that ridiculous purple blanket. "What's that you've got back there?" Her hand moves to her gun.

"A body," says Brian. "This is a mortuary transport van."

The officer says he better have paperwork and Brian says yes, of course, here is the paperwork. She reads it, then leans in close. "Your eyes look red, Mr. Lafferty. Have you consumed marijuana prior to operating this vehicle?"

"If you mean to ask if I'm high, the answer is no. I'm on call twenty-four seven, and I haven't slept since yesterday."

"You shouldn't be operating a motor vehicle if you're that tired."

"Someone's gotta drive the dead."

"Mr. Lafferty," she continues, "who are the two gentlemen with you?"

"New hires—bringing 'em out for a run. That one over there is fired." He points to Bill. "Got sick on the first day."

The officer lets out a little laugh.

"Excuse me, ma'am, but I'm in something of a hurry. That's a donor back there, headed to the operating room." He gestures over his shoulder to the body under the blanket.

"Wait here." She walks back to her patrol car, takes his driver's license and paperwork.

Ty's leg is cramping in the tight space, and the corpse next to him is starting to smell weird. "Is she going to arrest us?"

"For what?"

"I don't know—transporting human remains while stoned?"

"Just keep quiet. She's got no way to prove anything, and all my paperwork is in order. We're just a few guys out doing a job."

When she comes back to the van she leans in close again, gives Brian one last look. "Your license and paperwork check out. Whatever you guys are up to, be safe. We've got kids out here."

"Yes, ma'am."

The cruiser turns right out of the parking lot and Bill climbs back into the passenger seat. It's too much for him, too much for one day. And to make matters worse his mouth tastes like french fries and stomach acid. "Does anyone have any gum?"

Brian gives him two pieces. "You'll be fine. I puked all the time in Iraq. It was the heat." He laughs. "Hell, it feels kinda good after a while. Cleansing."

He calls from down the street. "It's Brian. I've got a drop-off."

They turn into a small driveway and a large garage door rolls open. He backs the minivan in and parks. "This is it. Keep your mouths shut."

Two technicians wearing dark blue scrubs and purple rubber exam gloves help Brian unload the gurney. After a quick inspection— they briefly unzip the plastic body bag to check the toe tag—there's the signing of some paperwork and then Brian is pulling himself into the van, lifting his banged-up body by the door handles.

"Easy," he says, and they're on their way, the garage door rolling shut behind them.

"I feel like a badass!" Ty bounces on the empty gurney. "I saw a dead body, even rode in a van right next to one, and I didn't puke!" He smiles at Bill and sticks his tongue out between straight, white teeth.

Bill's stomach is one big knot and he can't muster a response. Brian pulls into a gas station and buys him a ginger ale, tells him to drink it, he'll feel better. Bill takes a few sips and starts talking about how bad the Rockies are doing and soon he's feeling right again. "I can't imagine doing that, cutting out body parts for a living."

Ty says, "I bet they make bank."

"More than me." Brian unwraps another stick of gum. "But it's the people who run those places making the real money. Same as everywhere in America. That's why I've got my idea for the dog food shop."

Bill rolls his eyes. "You and that stupid dog food shop."

"You'll see, man. You'll see."

They're on Brian's couch again, the music playing. He loads another bowl and takes the first hit.

Ty reaches for the pipe and takes a puff. "So you just smoke weed all day and wait for the phone to ring—go out and pick up a dead body and drive it somewhere?"

"Yep, that's it. Smoke and play video games."

"And no one says anything?" He kicks his shoes off and leans back into the heavy cushions.

"Fuck no." Brian blows a thick column of smoke. "You know those guys in the blue scrubs? I've smoked weed right out behind the building with 'em. Shit, half of them are stoners and the other half are alcoholics. Ain't nothing pretty about their lives." He takes another hit before passing the pipe.

They're quiet for a minute, then Bill breaks the silence. "You should have seen that cop's face when she saw the body."

They all share a good laugh.

Ty thinks about Jackson in jail and asks Brian if he's heard the news.

"I told him not to go home with that girl. Poor dude—you guys visit him yet?"

Bill shakes his head. "We just found out today."

"I went last week—he didn't look so good. Like paranoid. Kept hushing me and telling me to be careful. He said the deputies knocked him around."

"Denver County is fucked." Ty takes a hit and passes.

"The sheriff resigned." Bill holds the pipe, waits for Ty to hand him the lighter. "And the feds found patterns of abuse."

"Won't do any good," says Brian. "Cops only care about cops."

Ty gets off the couch and paces on the dirty carpet. "Damn. We gotta make some money and get Jackson outta there."

"You guys ever heard of Boyztown?".

Bill says no but Ty smiles. "Boyztown, isn't that a gay strip club?"

"Yeah, you guys could put together a routine. I'm not sure they'll go for Bill—not much of a body—but Ty is a guaranteed hit."

"Fuck you, Brian." Bill is still shaken from his ordeal in the van. Ty grins.

Then Brian leans in like someone might be listening. "For real, you guys want to help out Jackson and make some money? I know someone who can help you."

"Who?" Ty raises an eyebrow.

"A friend of a friend—just chopped a big crop and needs help trimming. I know you fools can trim."

Bill leans back and crosses his arms in self-satisfaction. "We paid rent last month helping Kenny trim twenty pounds of Larry OG."

"Oh shit, I think I smoked that. Pretty dope."

"Kenny grows the dopest herb."

"Fucking Kenny."

"When are they trimming?" Bill takes another hit and feels his body relax.

"Tonight, man. They're going late—got a lot to get through."

Bill passes the pipe back. "What do you think, Ty?" He coughs. "You down for some trimming?"

Ty isn't sure. "Who is this guy?"

"I told you, a friend of a friend—a real funny Mexican guy by the name of Manny. He works out of the yellow house on 9th and Lipan. Knock on the door and say Brian sent you, he'll get you squared up."

"Okay, I'll do it for Jackson."

Brian's phone rings again. "Where? Denver Health? I'm leaving now." He puts the pipe down. "Got another run."

"No way," says Bill. "I'm not riding with another corpse. Fuck that."

"I'll drop you off along the way." Then he turns to Ty. "And for fuck's sake put your shoes back on."

5.

Jackson took his first pill in the dormitory of a New Mexico school for troubled teens. He was sixteen, and spent the night feverishly masturbating to a copy of Penthouse that he acquired from a old man outside a convenience store. Cost him twenty bucks but he got his money's worth.

The prescription drug habit fueled late-night study sessions, and Jackson's grades held steady into senior year. It was a fight in the cafeteria that got him expelled and sent back to his parent's house in military-populated Colorado Springs.

Soldiers can party, and he was quick to make friends. Supplying those friends with blow and pills was the perfect business, until the drugs became too much. He punched a bouncer at a local club and spent the night in the hospital getting stitched up. It was morning when the cell door slammed shut behind him. He sat on the concrete bench, knees pulled to his chest, and cried.

Dad hired a top defense attorney from Denver, who dressed him up in a dark grey suit and spoke to the judge about "unfortunate indiscretions" and "temporary setbacks." A week later he was on a flight to California, rehab, the charges dropped if he completed his stay. Morning yoga classes, walks along the beach, daily spa treatments, and meals prepared by an award-winning chef almost made up for the lack of pussy and cocaine.

It was a week before his discharge when dad called to say they would be expecting him in Colorado Springs. They had a room and could help with money.

"No," he said, "I'm not coming home." He took a bus to Denver, crashed on couches, got a job, bought a car, and found a place of his own—a rented house out in Lakewood with two roommates and a pit bull.

Now he's in jail again, knees pulled to his chest, locked in a smelly cell with the roaches and spiders. His cellmate is asleep in the bunk below, snoring and tossing from side to side. He stares at a thin crack in the concrete ceiling, imagines he might shrink down until he's small enough to pass through it, far away from this place of violence and intimidation and control.

In the morning he'll be shackled and stuffed into a van with ten desperate men and driven to the courthouse for a second hearing. The public defender will ask the judge to release him pending a trial, same as the last hearing, and the judge will say no. Then it's back into the shackles, back into the van, and back into the tiny cell with a cellmate who takes loud shits and paces naked in the dark. Another sleepless night staring at the crack in the ceiling.

He thinks of his mother and home and hot cinnamon rolls in the morning.

6.

Brian drops them on a busy corner on the south side of Denver Health Medical Center. Ty watches the black minivan disappear behind a smaller outbuilding. "I'm hungry."

"Let's go," says Bill, "it's not far."

They've made it three blocks when Ty spots a tiny silver trailer parked along the curb, still hitched to a beat-up Chevy Blazer. A chalk sign reads: TAMALES 3 FOR $5.

"Give me five bucks," he says. "Everyone knows these places have the dankest food." A heavy-set Mexican women with penciled eyebrows and pink cheeks takes cash from the small line of patrons at a cut-out window. "See," he says, pointing to the señora, "you can't argue with that."

Bill digs around for his last five dollar bill. "Get me chicken with red sauce."

He comes back with three foil-wrapped hot tamales. They stand on the sidewalk and eat, Ty going back to the counter to ask for a cup of water, Bill saying he's not thirsty then taking a sip from Ty's cup.

"Come on," he says, "we gotta get walking."

Ninth and Lipan. The last hint of summer sun disappears behind the mountains. They stand beneath a streetlight and deliberate.

"That's gotta be the place." Ty points to a yellow house three doors down, set back from a dingy picket fence. The porch is dark; the only light comes from a basement window.

"I don't know. What are we gonna do? Walk up and knock on the door?"

"Yeah, and tell them Brian sent us."

A man on a bicycle passes in the glow of a streetlight, one wheel squeaking with each slow revolution. At the next block he makes a u-turn and rides past again.

"I don't think anyone's home."

"Sure they are," says Ty. "They're in the basement. Kenny always trims in the basement."

Bill looks up and down the street. The man on the bicycle is gone. "Fuck it, let's get this over with."

They walk together past the picket fence, the old wooden porch sagging beneath them. Ty rings the doorbell. "For Jackson."

Bill nods. "For Jackson."

"What do you want?" The man standing in the open doorway is huge. Wide shoulders support a heavy neck and fat head, and he speaks English with a Mexican accent. "Who are you?"

"Brian sent us." Ty does his best to smile. "Said Manny needs help trimming."

"Brian said that?" The big man looks past them, leans out of the doorway and glances up and down the street. "Wait here."

They're standing on the dark porch when the man on the bike re-appears. He slows to watch them as he passes.

"Bill, that guy is making me nervous."

"Shhh, just be quiet and don't stare."

Five minutes pass. They hear footsteps and the door swings open. "Tell me your names," says the big man.

"I'm Bill, and the skinny guy next to me is Ty."

"Come in. Be quick."

They step inside the house and Bill makes small talk. "Nice to meet you. What's your name?"

But the big man doesn't answer. He leads them to a wooden staircase and they follow him down into the basement, the stairs moaning beneath their weight. A table in the center of the room is piled high with freshly cut marijuana.

"Brian sent you?" The voice is feminine, the accent Mexican, coming from a small man seated at the table.

"Yeah," says Bill. "We're friends."

"I called him. He vouched. Forgive me for not taking any chances."

"No problem."

"They call me Manny. And that gentleman over there is Raúl." He points to the big man who answered the door and then glances at the two seated beside him. "These are my cousins, Antonio and José."

"You guys need help? We can trim."

Manny looks at the weed and then back to where Bill and Ty are standing. He gestures to Raúl, who pulls a couple of chairs up to the table. "Sit," he says. "Let's see what you can do."

They sit. Ty grabs a pair of red-handled shears and picks through the sticky flowers.

"And don't be stingy. My customers expect quality."

They get to work trimming clean nugs and sorting them into plastic bins. The sight of so much weed on the table reminds Ty that his high is wearing off. The others, Manny and Raúl and the cousins, trim without speaking. Mexican soft rock plays on a small radio in the corner. Thirty minutes pass, and Ty is getting restless. "Manny," he says, "do think you could smoke us up?"

Manny doesn't look up from the table. "My friend, I welcomed you into my home. Now you insult me." There's the sound of his shears slicing through green stalks and stems. "What kind of a person do you think I am?"

"I'm sorry," says Ty. Bill kicks him beneath the table.

"Trim a few more pounds and I'll load that." He points to a huge glass bong on a low shelf, then looks at Raúl and giggles, a queer little burst of sound. "Keep them chasing the high, that's how you motivate stoners."

They continue trimming in awkward silence, Ty wishing he hadn't said anything and Bill wondering if Manny might want to kill them. The plastic bin between them is filling with marijuana, one neat little nug at a time. The only sound is the slicing of their shears and Mexican radio. But it doesn't take long for Ty to notice Raúl's breath, the air struggling to pass through that thick mass of neck and throat. Soon it's all he can hear, even the radio fades into the background of hot breath moving in and out, louder and louder. He imagines springing from his chair, running up the stairs and onto the street and away from the sound of the huge man. His thoughts are only interrupted by Manny's shears dropping to the table.

"So—" says Manny. "Now we smoke." He crushes loose buds between his fingers while José grabs the bong and a stick lighter.

Soon they're laughing, even Raúl and the cousins, and Ty is feeling better about everything.

"Oh, Shakira!" says Manny. "A mí me encanta Shakira!" He dances in his chair to the beat of the radio, raises his arms above his head and makes Shakira faces. They all laugh some more. "Tell me," he raises an eyebrow, "how do you guys know Brian?"

"Went to high school with a mutual friend," says Bill. "We've known him for years."

"Crazy fuck, all shot up in the war and driving bodies around in a minivan."

"Yeah, that's Brian."

"And he smokes like a chimney." Manny laughs. "Always good for business."

Ty holds up a fat nug. "How'd you start growing weed, Manny?"

Raúl and the cousins stop laughing. They look to their boss, wait to hear his reply to these dumb gringos.

Manny's expression becomes focused, stern. He takes the bong and draws a huge hit, holds it for a minute then blows a tight line of smoke from a pair of thin lips. "I'll tell you, but only because you know Brian." He pulls another long hit then passes the bong around the table. "Keep trimming."

They trim and Manny begins with the story of how he grew up in Mexico.

"When I was a boy," he says, "the other boys in school used to laugh at me and call me a maricón. Do you know that word, maricón?"

They shake their heads no.

"A very nasty word. In English it means something like faggot, and it should never be used for anyone, not even your enemy."

They nod in agreement and he continues. "Do you know what those boys would do to me? In the morning they made fun of my clothes, called me a girl, a fairy. At lunch they poured their sodas down the front of my pants; in the bathroom they pissed on my shoes. And after school, when the teachers weren't around to break things up, they'd beat me and steal my things. Once, they tore all of the clothes from my body and I stumbled naked and beaten through town. You should have seen my mother's face, seeing me come through the door covered in dirt and nothing else. And do you know what my father, the great man that he was, did to protect his son? Nothing. He did nothing. I overheard him telling my mother that a beating or two might do me good, might make me less of a maricón.

"What did I learn?" He doesn't wait for their reply. "I learned that the world is fucked. That nothing makes sense. Shit happens, and the system is corrupt. Why was I born a queer little boy in a dusty town in Mexico? Maybe it was to toughen me, to teach me things I never would have learned if I was born to privilege, or even worse, hetero-sexual.

"Things changed when I was eighteen. There was a young man in my town who worked for the cartel. Everyone knew it. He wore gold jewelry and rode a fast Kawasaki motorcycle. One day the police arrested him and held him in the little jail next to the courthouse in the center of town. A new judge was making a name for himself by waging a war on the cartel. This is what they did to the new judge: They pulled him from his bed while he slept, his fat wife screaming and clawing in the dark. They hung him upside down from a tree, naked, and cut his penis off with a dull blade. Then they poured gasoline over his body and lit him on fire. The new judge ordered the young man's release within a week. And there he was, buzzing the streets on his motorcycle, gold jewelry gleaming in the sun. It was then I decided to work in the drug business.

"But not like a cartel, mind you, with burnings and beheadings and the tiresome politics. No, that's not for me. My cousins were already in Denver, driving trucks back and forth to Kansas City. My aunt, their beautiful mother, has a house in Englewood and works for the university. That's how I came here." He stops and grins. "Not in the back of a truck, or wading through shit with garbage bags pulled over my legs. No, I came here on American Airlines, with a student visa and a thousand dollars in my wallet." He points to the cousins on either side of him. "These two picked me up at the airport."

He reaches for the bong and takes another rip. "I got a job working at a factory. A good job for someone with little English, making sixteen dollars an hour. So I worked the overtime shifts and slept in my aunt's basement and saved my money.

"Now you know what happens next? Some guy at the factory, some football-jersey-wearing asshole, follows me into the bathroom—comes right up behind me and slams me against the urinal. I don't know if he wants to rape me or kill me. And then he says, 'We don't want a wetback faggot like you working here. Go on back to Mex-zee-co and suck donkey dicks. This work is for real men.' Now here's the crazy part, the part you won't believe. That big, nasty, hairy man reached right around with his unmanicured hand and grabbed my cock and balls.

"You should know, gringos, that I'm normally a reasonable man. But when one trespasses against me as this man did, I'm prone to little fits. And that's what happened in that warehouse bathroom. I had a little fit. First, I slammed my head back into the man's face. I felt his nose break and there was blood. Some men, even hard men, see blood and go weak in the knees. This man, no surprise, was one of them. It was easy to knock him down. When they came rushing in I was on top of him, pounding his face where the nose was already broken. He kept his job and I lost mine. 'I gotta let you go,' said the manager. Said I'm lucky he didn't call the police. I'm lucky? What about the redneck who assaulted me? So even in the United States, like Mexico, the system is fucked."

He's silent for a moment as he stares at the green harvest before him. "That's when I knew I was ready to start growing."

"So he calls us," says Antonio, speaking for the first time all night.

"That's right," says Manny. "I call my scandalous cousins. The money I'd saved working in the factory went to a grow tent and twenty clones, with just enough left over for a used copy of Jorge's Bible. First crop was shit. But after that we got better. Wasn't long before I paid cash for this house and opened a second grow in the garage out back."

"Damn," says Bill. "You paid cash for this place?"

"Bought it cheap." Manny laughs. "There was a drive-by, one gang shooting up another. Some banger bled to death in the living room. You should have seen the carpet."

Ty's stomach tightens into a knot. "You're kidding, right?"

Manny shakes his head no. "Gang violence is such a pity, and terrible for real estate. Unless you want to buy a grow house."

Bill stares at the ceiling, imagines the blood pooling on the floor above him. Is that a dark spot?

Meanwhile, Manny loads another huge bowl, shakes a pinch of keef over the top. He takes the first hit and passes. One of the cousins disappears and returns with cold beer. They drink and smoke and trim.

"Oye—listen," says Manny. "In this country, the only problems are money problems. Every other problem can be paid for, negotiated, or imagined away. But you don't got money, you got all the problems in the world."

"Tell them about the apartments," says Antonio. "Tell them, Manny."

"Alright, alright. Keep quiet. Don't want to give these gringos all my secrets." He takes a sip of beer. "What does a dumb Mexican like me, a real ignorant Norteño from the desert, do with all that drug money? Fancy belt buckles and lowrider rims, right?"

Neither one of them dares to say anything.

"Well you're wrong, gringos." Manny smiles at the cousins and makes a self-satisfied expression. "I bought apartment buildings. Sixteen fucking apartment buildings."

"Sixteen apartment buildings?" Bill wishes he owned something—anything. "In Denver?"

"Pittsburgh."

Ty scratches his head. "Pittsburgh?"

"Yes, gringos. A delightful little city, Pittsburgh. Better known for football and the glory days of steel, these days it's undergoing something of a quiet renaissance. And the real estate—a real bargain, gringos. First time I went out there, I picked up a four-unit building for thirty grand and got hooked on it."

"And tell him, Manny," says Antonio. "Tell him the best part."

"Okay, okay. I've got all of my units rented Section Eight. Uncle Sam sends me a check every month to house the downtrodden, and I'm happy to do it. Even hired a property manager to run things for me, a little Thai woman named Porn. She's tough as nails, that Porn."

"Damn," says Bill. "That's genius."

"Yes." Manny takes another sip of beer and leans back in his chair. "Now you two gringos are here, trimming marijuana for me, a Mexican, while the United States Treasury sends me checks." Another sip of beer. "In Mexico they used to call me maricón."

The cousins nod their heads and Manny loads another bowl. "Trim faster, fuckers. You want to be here all night? Just you and the fucking spiders down here in the dark?"

The bong goes around again and they trim and Ty is thinking that Manny is one strange Mexican.

Bill is thinking about money. They've filled two plastic bins and the pile of weed on the table is not such a pile anymore. Damn it, he thinks, we should have cleared up payment at the beginning. But is he really so free to discuss terms, down here in the basement with a flaming Mexican and his pair of ox-sized cousins? It takes him another twenty minutes to work up the courage. "Manny, how much are you paying us for tonight?" He braces for a reaction.

But Manny is cool. "We're not finished."

"I know. I just want to know what you're paying us when the work is done."

"Damn," says Manny. "I'm hurt. You don't trust me?"

"It's not like that, Manny. It's just—"

"Here's the thing, gringo, we're not paying you for tonight."

"What?" Bill slams his shears down on the table.

"It's a trial run. Things works out, we'll be calling you."

"Brian didn't say anything about a trial run." He pushes his chair back and stands. "This is bullshit!"

Now José, silent all night, stands up across the table. "Go easy, gringo. Better sit back down and act nice."

But Bill doesn't sit. He surveys the room—sees Ty squeezing his knees the way he always does when he's nervous, Antonio and José nodding and saying be cool. It's another minute before he lowers himself into the chair and looks at Manny, his heart thumping in his chest.

Manny is still cool. "Do you feel better after shouting in my basement?"

"He's sorry," says Ty. "Real sorry."

"That wasn't my question." Manny takes a long sip of his beer and asks again, "Do you feel better?"

Bill works to control his breath. "Yes, I feel better."

"That's what I thought. Now be nice."

"If you're not paying us then we're leaving. Let's go, Ty."

Ty is still holding his shears. He wants to go with Bill, to stand and leave the house, but he can only sit and trim.

Manny smiles. "Looks like your friend doesn't want to leave."

Bill takes the shears from the table and goes back to work. Snip. Snip. The metal slices through crisp stems with little bursts of anger.

The cousins stop their trimming to watch. Manny says, "Trim my weed with love. Don't be angry, gringo."

But Bill stiffens up, his face hard. Then the Mexicans explode with laughter, grabbing their stomachs and shouting at each other in Spanish.

Manny rolls back in his chair. "I'm fucking with you, gringo! We'll pay you, okay? We'll pay you." He opens another beer. "Two hundred and fifty each plus an ounce of tree—the best of the crop. You guys are solid trimmers. Sound good?" Then he hands the open beer to Bill and says, "Here, gringo, drink this."

Bill takes a deep sip. "Fuck, that's messed up." He works to conceal his anger, let's out a nervous chuckle.

"We feel out all the new guys." Manny laughs again. "I'm impressed, gringo. You stood up to me. Not many stoners have the balls. Maybe you're a little bit Mexican after all."

"We need the money for our friend in jail."

"Oh, shit! Oye!" Manny claps his hands. "My uncle Oscar is a bail bondsman."

"Yeah?"

"Got an office on Delaware right next to the jail. I'll call him—he answers for me twenty-four hours a day."

"We don't have the money," says Ty. "We've got to trim a lot more weed."

"It's five grand," says Bill, "the bail."

Manny slams his open hands on the table. "Oh, you gringos don't know anything! I come to this country from a shithole village in Mexico and I know more about how things work than you dumb Americans. Did you even go to school?" He pauses to take a sip of beer then laughs again, the frothy liquid spitting out between his lips. "The bondsman puts up the bail money for a ten percent fee. You only need five hundred. You want me to call Oscar? He doesn't mind working late for a buck."

Ty jumps up and down in his seat. "Yes, call Oscar!" He looks at Bill. "Call Oscar, right?"

"Right," says Bill. "We're busting Jackson out tonight."

"Oh, gringos!" Manny clasps his hands together. "I'm inspired. Truly. Such friendship. You finish trimming—I'm not paying a cent until the work is done—and I'll make the call." Antonio hands him a cell phone and he disappears up the stairs. They hear him in the kitchen, pacing and speaking Spanish.

Antonio opens another beer and hands it to Ty. "Hey, you're doing a good thing taking care of your friend. It shows loyalty, the most important trait of any real man."

"Thanks."

"You stay loyal to Manny like you stay loyal to your friend, understand? You stay loyal to Manny and good things will happen to you." He stares at Ty, eyes narrowing to little slits.

"Okay." The quiet man still makes him a little nervous.

"Good."

They clink beers and drink together.

The wooden staircase creaks under Manny's shoes as he slinks back down the steps. He's holding two white envelopes. "It's settled, Oscar will meet you at his office in an hour. It's not far. In the meantime you can help us finish up." He hands them each an envelope. "Payment for a job done. I had fun with you gringos. Oh, I almost forgot—your marijuana." He goes to a row of purple plastic bins lining the wall. "Do you want Blue Dream or Thunder Fuck? Maybe a little of both?"

"Yeah." Ty giggles. "A little of both."

Manny tosses them each a plastic bag of green, tightly-trimmed buds. "You've got the Blue Dream, Ty. That's the good stuff."

They finish the last of the trimming and empty their beers. Mexican rock still plays on the radio, sounding better with each pass of the bong. Soon they're shaking hands, saying goodbye to the cousins, and following Manny up the stairs.

Ty rubs his tired eyes. "What time is it?"

"After midnight, better get going." Manny opens the front door. A moth dances around the porch light.

Ty looks up and down the street. He remembers the man on the bike. "Manny, there was a man earlier, on a bike—"

"You mean Candelario?" Manny stares out into the dark. "I give him marijuana and cheap beer and a little money for groceries and he watches the neighborhood for me—gives me a call anytime the cops cruise through. I knew you gringos were coming before you rang the doorbell."

"Damn," says Bill. "That's gangster shit."

"Sí," says Manny, "gangster shit."

The same gray moth is still beating against the porch light when Bill and Ty leave the yellow house and the glow of the streetlight and follow the cracked sidewalk into the night. Ty is sure he hears a bicycle, the squeaking of a wheel turning slowly in the distance.

7.

Oscar Martinez sits in his office in a tiny wooden house painted blue with "Martinez Bail Bonds" in big yellow letters on the side—on a block across from the jail where all the old houses have been turned into bail offices. He sips whiskey from a flask and waits for two gringos, sent by his nephew Manny to get a five-thousand dollar bond.

He's tired. He spent last night in the car, parked down the street from a bail skipper's last known residence. Five coffees and a box of donuts later the sun comes up and still no fugitive. There's a picture of the man—kid, really—on his desk, arrested for selling ecstasy tablets at a nightclub. Oscar will find him eventually, probably hiding out with his stringy girlfriend, scared shitless about prison. Oscar Martinez has seen a thousand kids like this one.

There's another picture on his desk. It's his mother, widowed, still living with extended family in Mexico. He sends her five hundred dollars every month by MoneyGram.

"Mamá," he tells her, "come to the United States and live with us. There's an extra room in the house." But she always says no, she will never leave Mexico. Americans are too cold, too indifferent.

His thoughts are interrupted by the buzzer. He takes another sip of whiskey and slides the flask into a desk drawer next to an old scratched-up, nickel-plated revolver.

"I'm coming." He walks, in no particular hurry, to the door.

PLEASE RING BELL FOR SERVICE, reads a cracked plastic sign above the buzzer.

Ty presses the button. "Do you think it's working?"

Bill says, "I don't know. Press it again."

Ty presses the buzzer again, mashes it down with his hand. The door jerks open and he takes a step back, startled by the man in the open doorway.

"Excuse you," says the man, "buzzer works just fine."

"I'm sorry," says Ty. "It's getting chilly. You Oscar?"

He nods. "You the boys sent over by Manny?"

"Yeah. We're here to bail our friend Jackson out of jail."

"A girl?"

"No. Jackson's a guy."

Oscar shrugs. "Never can tell these days. Come on in."

They sit in Oscar's office at the back of the little blue house. He brings them hot coffee in styrofoam cups and gives them a clipboard with forms to fill out. "Because you know Manny," he says, "I'll waive the extra paperwork fee."

They pool the cash from their envelopes and stack it neatly on the desk in front of him. He thumbs through the bills and when he's satisfied he says, "Okay, I'll make the call to the jail and get things started." Then he slides open the center desk drawer, fumbles through junk until he finds a thin blunt. "Let's smoke to your friend." There's the flash of a lighter and he's taking a long hit, holding it in then blowing a thick column of smoke. He passes the blunt to Ty and goes into the next room.

Ty takes a hit. "It's magical, bro. Magical."

"Huh?"

"Just think, we started the day with no weed and a friend in jail. Now we're here, in a bail bondsman's office, our pockets stuffed with herb and a burning blunt in our hands. Good things happen, Bill. Good things happen." His eyes are tiny slits, the lids drooping.

Bill takes a hit. "I guess so." The room fills with the skunky-sweet smell of marijuana and cherry-flavored blunt wrapper.

"Bad news, boys." Oscar appears in the doorway. They watch him come around the desk and take his seat. "The bond will go through alright, but your friend ain't gettin' out tonight."

"What happened?"

"It's a damn shame, I was starting to like you boys. Pass me that blunt." He takes a quick hit, then another. "Jackson's been transferred out to the county jail."

"I don't understand," says Bill. "What does that mean?"

"It means he's no longer downtown. All the inmates who can't make bail get shipped out to county. And there's one other thing."

"What?"

"Your friend has to wear an alcohol-monitoring ankle bracelet while he's out on bail. And the guy who does the ankle bracelet fittings doesn't come back to work until Monday. That means your friend will get out on Tuesday, maybe Wednesday."

"Damn," says Bill, "that sucks."

Ty imagines Jackson wearing a court-ordered ankle bracelet and laughs. "He'll look so hood, yo."

Bill chuckles. "So hood."

"Glad you boys are taking it well. The good news is that I'll file the paperwork tonight. Get the ball rolling."

Ty decides he likes Oscar. He looks around the room and notices a pair of handcuffs on a shelf beside a can of pepper spray. "What are those for?"

"Runners," says Oscar. "Gotta hook 'em up and bring 'em back to court or I lose my bond money."

"Like Dog the Bounty Hunter?"

Oscar laughs. "Yeah, like Dog the Bounty Hunter. Matter of fact, Dog got his start right here in Denver—on this very street. Even hauled in a runner or two for me back in the day."

Ty is thrilled. Bill is less impressed, keeps his head down, works his way through the stack of paperwork for Jackson's bond.

"What's the craziest thing you've ever seen?"

Oscar takes another hit and thinks for a moment. "Well, let's see— I've been shot at five times. Hit with a bat twice. And once this cow of a woman came at me with a hot iron, swinging it over her head by the electrical cord, on account of I went to arrest her husband.

"Now most people take it okay. As soon as I say, 'you're under arrest,' their bodies just go limp.

"But then you've got the people who want to give me lip, make threats, or do something really stupid like pull a gun. It takes balls to deal with those people. But I've got a few tricks up my sleeve, like a million volt stun gun I bought at a police supply store. And my poker buddy Ronnie is a cop. I can't believe they let that dumbshit redneck wear a badge and carry a gun—always talking about how he can't wait to use it.

"Yep—I've seen just about everything there is to see. People coming to the door naked, dripping with sweat and sex. Drugs. Kids left to hang around in their own filth. Hell, I even found a dead guy. See, I rang the doorbell and stood on the porch for a minute or two, and all the while this awful smell is just building. So I go around to a side window and peek into the living room. Poor bastard's rotting away in an overstuffed easy chair. Never did get my bond money."

"Awesome!" Ty imagines himself riding with Oscar, chasing dangerous fugitives through seedy alleyways. Finally, a job that doesn't sound boring.

"Don't get the wrong idea, kid. Most of the time it's just waiting around, or doing paperwork at one in the morning while my wife sleeps alone."

"Do you think I could ride with you to catch a fugitive?"

"Well that depends, kid. Are you any good in a fight?"

Bill looks up from the paperwork. "He's never been in one."

"That's not true. What about Nick Lambert?"

"You were both so drunk you just rolled around in the dirt until we threw water on you. That's not a fight."

"Well can you stay awake all night to keep watch?"

Bill scoffs. "Are you kidding? He's the only person I know who can walk and fall asleep at the same time."

"Well then, can you at least roll the joints?"

Ty bounces in his chair. "Yes—I can do that!"

"Take a card, kid. I like you." He hands Ty the card and goes for a handshake. "That's not how you do it, kid. Here—get a strong grip like this."

Then Bill says he's finished with the paperwork and Oscar takes the file and thumbs through each page.

"Looks good," he says. "I'll give you a call Monday, let you know when your friend is due to be released." He rubs beneath his tired eyes.

Ty pulls out his sack of weed and sets a big fat nug on the desk. "For the help with our friend, and the blunt."

"Thanks, kid. You remember to look me up. And say hello to Manny for me next time you're out that way." He leans across the desk. "Hey kid, did Manny go for you? You know, make a pass?"

"What?" Ty is confused.

"You're his type, you know. Manny loves the skinny white boys." He picks the nug off the desk, rotates it in his hand, brings it to his nose. "Just imagine poor Manny back in Mexico, in that little village, watching California boys like you on his mother's little television set. It's no wonder—"

"No, he didn't make a pass." Ty considers it for a moment. "I don't think he wanted me like that."

"Oh, you'd know. Nothing subtle about Manny."

"Well," says Bill, "this has been fun." The marijuana and the beer and the walking and these Mexicans with their sense of humor have all been too much for him. "It's late. We have to go."

"You know I got out of bed for you, gringo. Left my wife alone with the kids in a big house."

"Yes, I know. And we're grateful, Oscar. I'm grateful. It's just that it's been a long day and my head is beginning to ache, and we've got a long walk home."

Oscar grumbles a little more as he shows them to the front door. He gives Bill a stiff handshake, slaps Ty hard on the shoulder. "You remember to say hello to Manny for me."

They're down the steps, on the sidewalk, when the door slams shut behind them.

"Why'd you have to be a jerk?"

"I'm tired."

"You're always a jerk when you're tired."

"Look, Ty. Can we just walk home, please?"

"I can't believe you." Ty is walking next to him, arms waving as he talks. "Aren't you even the least bit excited?"

"About what?"

"Getting the money for Jackson in one day? I mean, our friends knew for a week. A week! And all those guys with their money couldn't come through. But we came through, Bill. We came through."

"Some friends we have, huh?"

"There you go again." Ty throws his hands up. "Always being so negative, like when that stupid magazine didn't want to publish your story and you stopped writing."

"Low blow, asshole. Besides, the editor of that stupid magazine is retarded."

"I don't think you're supposed to say retarded anymore. Like, it's a bad word or something."

"I'm a writer. I can say whatever the fuck I want."

"I know what you need to lighten the mood. Benny Blanco's—open late."

"I'm tired, Ty."

"Come on, man! We're stoned as fuck, and greasy pizza is just a few blocks over. Let's celebrate getting our best friend out of jail."

"I wouldn't say best friend—"

"Bill!"

"Alright, little Ty-bot. Let's get pizza. How could I resist that face?"

So they stand on the corner of 13th and Pearl, eating huge slices of thin crust pizza, drinking root beer from the can. A group of bikers on Harley's roll past, a late night cruise, hot exhaust blowing up dust from the street.

"You're right," says Bill. "Today was a good day." He lifts the can to his lips, chugs the last of his root beer. "I'm going back for another. You want one?"

Ty smiles and nods.

"Wait here. I'll be right back."

He waits beneath the streetlight, chewing his crust.

8.

Joe is hungry. He hasn't had a real meal in two days. The drugs aren't selling—not like they used to—since the dispensaries took all the pot business from the street dealers. If it wasn't for the pharmaceuticals, addictions to Oxycontin and Xanax, he'd starve. You can always count on the pharmaceuticals; they don't take long to sell. If only he had a bottle of Percocet right now, or even just a few pills, he'd be filling his belly at the diner.

Instead he's slogging through alleys, lifting dumpster lids in search of his next meal. His favorite spot behind the Mexican restaurant on 6th turns up dry—not a single wrapped burrito or even an edible pile of beans. It's not my night, he thinks. Hell, it's not even my year.

Maybe the Japanese place on Colfax threw away some egg rolls? People hate soggy egg rolls. He walks back up Pearl towards Uptown, head low and feet shuffling along. His body is tired and his knees ache.

He's ready to give up on dinner when he sees a familiar face standing alone beneath a streetlight, eating a piece of pizza crust. And the hunger in Joe's stomach flares. His vision goes blurry. He can't speak. There's only the yellow light, and the skinny man with the blonde hair licking grease off his lips.

Ty tucks the last piece of crust into his mouth and makes a satisfied smack as he licks his thumb. Where's that napkin? He reaches into his pocket and comes out empty-handed. Something isn't right. The sack of weed Manny gave him is gone. "Bill!" he shouts. Where's Bill?

His heart races. He thinks of where he's been, retraces his steps, struggles under the fog of too much weed to remember. Bill is going to kill him.

He's too confused to notice the strange figure approaching—doesn't see the man brace and lunge forward until it's too late. Then he's on the ground, his arm burning, the breath knocked from his chest. He reaches for his elbow and feels warm, wet blood. "What the fuck, man?"

"Didn't want to buy my drugs—couldn't even spare me a dollar."

"I don't want any trouble. I just want to go home."

Joe takes a step closer, twisted shadows falling across his face. "How 'bout you give me some money so I can get a slice?"

"I would—I would give you money for pizza, but I don't have any. Not even a dollar." He pulls his pockets inside out. "Lost a bag of pot, too."

"Maybe you're lying to me. Maybe I should just beat your skinny ass."

"No—I wouldn't lie to you." He imagines Bill finding him broken and bruised in the street—no wallet, no money, no weed. "Please don't hit my teeth," he says, trying to stand.

But before he can straighten up, the crazy street dealer reaches out with a dirty hand and grabs him by the shirt.

Ty stumbles backward. His shirt tears free from the man's grip and he runs—runs for his life. His heart beats against his ribs. Where the fuck is Bill?

"Bill!" he cries. "Bill!"

He turns to look back and trips, falls to the crumbling sidewalk and scrapes his palms. Then he's up and running again. A hard left into the alley. A dumpster. Hide behind the dumpster. He crouches down, listening to his own breath, loud and rattling, a dead give-away in the night. Quiet, he thinks. Fucking quiet.

Footsteps—a boot splashes in a watery pothole. "I hear you breathing back there," says the crazed man. "Why can't you just give me a dollar?"

Ty steps out from behind the dumpster. Tears stream down his face. "I told you," he screams, "I don't have a dollar!" He brings both hands together in front of him, pleading. "I don't have a fucking dollar!"

Bill shuffles around beneath the streetlight, drinking his root beer. A second can, the one he bought for Ty, is stuffed in his back pocket. It's late. Where did Ty go?

He sits on a graffitied bench and notices a scrap of fabric on the dirty pavement. He nudges it with his toe, bends over to pick it up. It's a piece of Ty's shirt, faded and thin. "Ty!" he shouts. "Ty!"

Now he's running down the dark street, peering into each door-way, every alley. He drops the can of soda and doesn't stop to pick it up. The sidewalks are uneven, cracked. He trips once, then again, but keeps going. A block. Then two. There's a long alley and at the far end he sees two figures in the dark. "Ty!"

"I told him I don't have a dollar!" Ty's face is covered in sloppy tears, glistening in the light of a moldy utility lamp.

The man drops low, rushes Ty at the waist and pins him into the dumpster.

"Do something!"

But Bill can only stand and watch.

It feels good, breaking this punk's body against the dumpster. It's been too long since he gave anyone a good beating. And now—now he thinks he might just kill the little bitch—smash his face in like he should have done to the punk who jumped his brother. He takes another jab at the ribs and feels the skinny hipster crumple. He pulls back and lands a hard punch to the gut. His body fills with rage, the release of years of frustration and hopelessness and hunger.

Now the other hipster, the boyfriend in the stupid jacket, is pleading for his skinny lover. Joe thinks he'll kill that one, too. Then he hears the man say, "I'm sorry," and he stops hitting and punching.

"I'm sorry," the man says again. "I'm sorry for telling you to fuck off."

"What did you say to me?"

"I said I'm sorry. We're sorry—we should have helped you out with a dollar."

Now it's Joe who can't move, trying to remember the last time someone apologized to him for something, anything. But he can't remember.

His arms drop. He looks at the person in front of him, sees tears and a frightened face and realizes he's the cause of it. Oh no, he thinks, what the fuck have I done?

9.

Jackson's awake, hiding beneath a thin and scratchy blanket, listening to his fat cellmate take a morning shit. With no ventilation in the tiny concrete cell, the smell will linger for hours. But breakfast will come soon, and laundry duty after that.

But this morning is different. He's eating breakfast at the usual table when a sour deputy puts a hand on his shoulder. "Come on. Let's go."

"Go where?"

"Don't argue with me, inmate." The grip on his shoulder tightens. "Transfer. Back downtown."

"Now?"

The deputy makes an ugly face.

"Don't I get to say goodbye?" Jackson can't imagine wanting to leave a place any more than jail, but he's sad to leave the friends he's made—the people who've helped him survive his short time inside.

"This isn't summer camp, damn it. Let's get moving."

"Alright—alright." He walks slowly, makes the deputy wait.

There's the search, the rough hands, the tightening of the shackles, then he's in another white van with another crew of desperate men. This time he's lucky; he got the window seat.

It's an hour-long ride through traffic to the Downtown Detention Center. They unload, more rough hands and searches and paperwork.

He sits in a holding cell for thirteen hours with a rotating assortment of Denver's broken, scared, and just plain stupid. Finally, the deputies come for him and he's trading one cell for another. There's the heavy clink of the door and again he's waiting.

His temporary cellmate is a sickly-looking guy named Gus, an old man with grey, thinning hair and a fiberglass cast on his right wrist. Gus says he was dumpster diving, stacking anything of value into the bed of his rusty pickup, when he was approached by the police.

"He asks me what I'm doing," says Gus. "So I tell him I'm earning my dinner—and recycling." He laughs. "He must have thought I was being smart because the next thing I know he's slamming me into the asphalt, yelling at me to stop resisting. But I wasn't resisting him none."

"Is that what happened to your arm?"

"Oh, this?" He raises the cast. "They did this here—where they knew the cameras weren't watching. Fucking deputy cranked my arm up behind my back so hard he snapped my wrist. Wrote up a nice report explaining how I was resisting his commands and throwing blows. But how could I punch anyone with four deputies on my back? Now I'm headed to prison for assaulting an officer."

"Damn," says Jackson. "That's some serious shit."

"Pretty serious, brother. Pretty serious."

Two days later he meets with a case manager who tells him he'll be getting released in two more days, on Thursday, when the electronic monitoring officer can make an appointment to fit his alcohol-monitoring bracelet.

"Alcohol-monitoring bracelet?"

"Yes, the one you'll be wearing twenty-four hours a day as a condition of your pretrial release," she says. "It reads the sweat from your skin and reports backs if you consume any alcohol. The judge ordered it."

He remembers when his friend Devin did six months of house arrest for a second graffiti offense. The curfew cut into happy hour but the ankle bracelet was a major hit with the ladies.

"You'll need a permanent address," she says, "a place where you can stay. Any questions?"

He says no, no questions, and is escorted back to his cell by two particularly boring deputies. Two more days with Gus and his broken wrist, two more days eating shitty food and wearing shitty clothes, surrounded by insanity, smothered by the system, with nothing to do but watch a spider in her web, waiting, like him.

Release day comes. More searches, handcuffs, sterile hallways, and standardized paperwork. Then he's at a metal desk, a detention deputy sitting on the other side. His clothes are returned one item at a time.

The deputy says, "We don't have your shoes."

"What? I don't understand."

"Something happened." The deputy's expression is flat and unconcerned. "Your shoes are missing. We don't have them."

"You lost my fucking DC's?"

"Language, inmate."

"I don't believe this—what am I supposed to do without shoes?"

"That's not really the sheriff's problem."

He changes into his clothes and signs a form and they take him to another office where he sits in another crappy plastic chair. There's a man wearing a blue dress shirt and a red tie. His head is bald, not the rough stubble bald of a guy who shaves his head, but the smooth and polished bald of a man who can't grow hair.

"I'm Dennis," says the bald man, "your pretrial electronic monitoring officer." He looks down at Jackson's socks. "Something happen to your shoes?"

Jackson shrugs.

"Pull a sock down. Let's get your bracelet on."

Jackson slinks back in the chair, puts his foot up on the corner of the desk and watches Dennis tighten the thick plastic strap around his ankle.

"There," says Dennis, "all set."

Then it's one last door and a deputy says, "Good luck."

10.

Don Ulibarri looks at his gold watch. "Hal, when's this stupid thing gonna be over?"

"Come on, Don. We gotta get it right. One more take."

"You've said 'one more take' fifteen times already. I'm getting hungry. Didn't they used to cater these things?"

"Budget cuts."

"Well if the director didn't want so many takes—"

"Damnit, Don. Just read the fucking lines."

Don turns to face the camera and smiles wide. "Like this?"

"Read the lines."

"Hi, folks. I'm Don Ulibarri, two-time Denver Broncos Super Bowl Champion. Nothing makes YOU feel like a champ more than a new car or sport utility! So rush on down to Ulibarri Motor City, where you don't need a Super Bowl ring to get VIP service!" He waves to the camera, two gold rings on his pudgy fingers. "You fucking happy?"

Hal shakes his head, crosses his arms. "You been drinking today, Don?"

"What are you gonna do, fire me? Last time I checked, it's my name on the sign out there."

"Alright, take it easy. We're done."

"Was that so fucking hard?"

"Don't kill anyone on the way home, asshole."

11.

Ty's ribs ache. The ice pack isn't doing much to help. "Bill, I need more weed!"

Bill brings fresh ice from the freezer and grinds another bowl. A skunky haze fills the apartment. "It's just a few bruises. You'll be fine."

"At least now I can tell Oscar I've been in a real fight."

Bill snorts. "Yeah, and you would've lost if I hadn't apologized."

"How'd you know that's all he wanted to hear?"

"I didn't." He shrugs. "But when I'm mad, I'm usually just looking for an apology. Anyway, I'm glad it worked."

Ty takes a huge hit. "You know—" Cough. Cough. "I kinda feel sorry for him."

"Who?"

"Joe. He's out there on the street in the cold and the snow and the rain." He hands the pipe back.

Bill waves it off. "You finish the bowl and I'll grind another before I leave."

"Where are you going?"

"To find a job." He frowns. "Before we're sleeping next to Joe."

Bill sits at a plain metal desk. There's a man in a white shirt on the opposite side, going over his application for employment.

"It says here," the manager clears his throat, "that your last position was at a bread factory—seven months ago."

"That's right. I took some time off to write a novel."

"And your novel, has it been published?"

"Not yet. I'm still shopping it around."

"I see," says the manager. "What makes you interested in customer service? We're looking for a specific type of personality, a real people person."

"Well, that's just it," says Bill. "After all that time in seclusion, I'm in need of human interaction. I love people. Bring on the people." He wonders if the lie is visible on his face.

The manager seems unconcerned. "Here's the deal: I've got a part-time position open on weekends. You'll have to be available the rest of the week in case we need you, but you won't get paid unless you come in. No benefits are offered, not unless you get a full-time position, which—I'm only being honest—are reserved for management. You'll start with a two-day orientation class, and if you pass the training we'll add your name to the schedule."

"What's the pay?"

"Nine dollars an hour, but after six months of probation it jumps up twenty-five cents. Oh, and you have to buy your own uniform shirts—we've got it set up to come out of your first paycheck. Any more questions?"

"Nope," he says. "You've pretty much covered things."

12.

Oscar Martinez reaches into a desk drawer, fishes his hand around, comes out holding a sack of weed. He packs some loose bud into a small pipe and takes a hit, sits back in his office chair. Maria would never allow it in the house, he thinks, not with the baby around. Just dumb luck the kid forgot his sack.

The phone rings. "Hello, Martinez Bail Bonds. What? Your son got caught with what? Oh, yes—that's a very serious charge, ma'am. Why don't you come in right away and we'll start the paperwork? Yes, I'll be here."

Oscar hangs up the phone, takes another hit and holds it in a long time before blowing out the smoke in one slow, thin exhalation. As long as drugs are illegal, he thinks, I'll be in business.

13.

Vicky Pulaski steers her red Subaru with one hand, holds her cell phone with the other. She turns south on Broadway at 11th Avenue. "I know, mom," she says into the phone, "I'm staying out of trouble. What? No—I won't see those people again."

She crosses two lanes of traffic, cuts off a Jeep in the middle lane and the driver honks. She drops the phone into her lap and slams down on the horn, flips him off as she swerves around him. "What the fuck?"

She goes back to steering with her left hand and picks up the phone. "Sorry, mom. What's that? No, everything's fine—just some rude man in traffic. Yes, I got the check that dad sent. What? Oh yes, tell him thanks."

She pulls into a gas station, gets out to fuel up. "I promise. Yes, I'm being good." She tries to unscrew the gas cap and it won't budge. "Look mom, I've got to go. I'm getting gas, okay?" She hangs up the phone and tries with both hands, but the cap still won't turn.

"Need help?" The voice comes from a man on a green metal bench.

"No, thanks." She doesn't like the look of his tattered clothes, the smell of alcohol.

"I won't hurt you, miss. I only aim to help." He walks over to where she's standing and she takes two quick steps to the side. He twists the gas cap with a wiry hand and it comes free. "There," he says, "the summer heat expands the metal."

"Oh." She takes the handle from the pump, lifts the lever. "Excuse me."

He steps out of her way. "Miss, you wouldn't happen to have a dollar you don't mind parting with?"

"That's what this was about? Get lost."

He shuffles back to his bench and sits, scratches the side of his head.

Inside the convenience store she says to the disinterested clerk behind the counter, "There's a man out there begging your customers for money."

"He's on the sidewalk," says the clerk. "Ain't nothing illegal about sitting on the sidewalk."

"It's bad for business—these nasty bums. Someone should do something about it, round them all up or something."

"Yes, ma'am."

She pulls up outside the little apartment building, looks for an address, honks the horn. A few seconds later the door opens, Jackson waves and says he'll be out in a minute. She watches him walk to the car, his baggy white t-shirt hanging over a loose pair of khaki shorts, the monitoring bracelet bulging on one ankle. "Damn, babe," she says as he climbs into the car, "you look hot."

"Yeah, it's like ninety degrees out here." He wipes the sweat off his forehead with the sleeve of his t-shirt.

"No, silly. I meant sexy."

"Thanks." He laughs. "How you been?" "Dad bailed me out—been gettin' by. How 'bout you?"

"Jail sucked." He reaches down, scratches beneath the itchy plastic bracelet.

"I'm sorry." She curls her lips into a little pout, puts her hand on his thigh and slides it up towards his crotch. "I've got something for you."

"Oh yeah? What about lunch?"

"Jackson! Always thinking with your stomach."

They make their way back to her place, stopping first at a drive-thru window to pick up lunch—Jackson ordering three hamburgers, two apple pies, and a milkshake. She pays and he eats an apple pie in the passenger seat.

"Slob." She laughs at the chocolate milkshake all over his lips.

Inside the dirty apartment, he sprawls out on the couch and eats a hamburger. She goes to the kitchen and comes back a few minutes later with a rolled joint, holds it out to him. "Did I do okay?"

"It's a little crooked, but you did okay." He eats until the food is gone and the joint is burned downed to a little roach.

Vicky sits on the couch next to him and rubs his back. "Feel good?"

"Mhmm." He slides forward onto his belly. "Amazing."

"I want to do anything I can—" She pauses. "—to make you feel good." She pulls at his shoulder, gets him to roll up and lean back against the couch. Her hand goes to his crotch and she strokes, up and down, while the other hand pulls down his shorts.

"Damn, Vicky."

"Don't you want me to?"

"Yes. Fuck yes."

Her lips slide over his throbbing cock, tongue tickling the foreskin until her mouth consumes his thick shaft—Jackson moans and arches his back. She slides a hand down his leg, finds the ankle bracelet and wraps her fingers around the awkward shape. He groans. Now she's as horny as he is, the tension building inside of her until she's climbing on top of him, riding him up and down until they both collapse in a pile of sweat and sex and exhaustion.

"What was that for?"

"You turn me on so much, my sexy bad boy."

He smirks. "That's me."

"But what if you could commit one crime and never need money again?"

"You mean like a big score?"

"Yeah, well—it's just that—when I was in jail, locked up with all those women and not a real man in sight, I heard a lot of stories. Most of those women, well they did something stupid, like they stole food at the grocery store or violated probation or something."

"Yeah, what's your point?"

"Well, I started thinking." She moves closer until her naked thighs are pressed against his and she rubs his neck and shoulders. "If you're gonna break the law, why not go for a big hit, get set for life?"

"Where'd you get that idea, some Hollywood movie?"

"What does it matter?" She kisses his neck and nibbles at his ear.

"You got any ideas?"

"I don't know," she says. "But you gotta plan it right, go for the big money without getting killed or busted. Low risk, high reward."

"You're serious?"

"Well—"

"Vicky! Don't you think I'm in enough trouble?"

"That's just it," she says. "You're already an outlaw—got that bracelet strapped to your ankle and a felony drug charge pending. Who's gonna hire you? But what if you never had to take orders from anyone ever again—not even your family?"

"Go on."

14.

"Don? Don Ulibarri?" The voice comes up from behind. Probably another fan. They're always bothering him for autographs and these days, the fuckin' selfies.

"Yes?" He spins around. "Autograph?"

"I'm here for Tony Giannopoulos."

"Oh, I see." He had hoped it would be another week or two before Tony's men came looking.

"Tony wants to know what happened to his money."

"Nothing—alright? I've got it—all of it."

"Prove it."

"What? You crazy? I don't carry that kind of cash around."

"You got one week."

"Huh?"

"One week," says the man, "to come up with the money, or Tony ain't gonna be so friendly."

"Don't you know who I am?"

"You won the Super Bowl—some quarterback or something."

"Twice. I won the Super Bowl twice, and I don't appreciate threats."

"Who's making threats?" The man smiles. "You got one week." Then he's gone, another stranger on a busy sidewalk.

Don wipes his sweaty palms on a pair of cheap polyester pants, pulls a pack of cigarettes from a pocket and fumbles for a lighter.

15.

Bill shares a small plastic table with a coworker in a blue shirt. The human resources manager bobs in and out of the room, switching the outdated video tapes that all new hires are made to sit through.

"Employee engagement," says the smiling man on the video, "means that every employee is behind our company's mission, that every action you take is in alignment with our customer service vision."

Bill chuckles to himself. "For nine dollars an hour, who the fuck are they kidding?"

The other guy laughs. "I know, right?"

"Hey, you wanna get stoned at lunch?"

"Sure."

The tape ends and they wait for the manager but she doesn't come. Bill wanders out into the hall and another employee tells him the manager went to lunch, and they should go to lunch, too. So they walk together to a pizza joint in a little strip-mall across from the store. Bill gets a slice of cheese and Ryan—the other guy's name tag says Ryan—orders pepperoni. They eat greasy slices from paper plates in the back alley and Bill lights a joint.

"How'd you wind up here?"

"At the store?" Ryan takes a hit and holds it. "Second job," he says, the smoke billowing out between his lips. "I drive a dump truck full-time. Got another kid on the way and it's not enough. What about you? You seem smart. How'd you wind up in a shithole like this?"

"I'm a writer," says Bill.

Ryan laughs. "I get it."

"Gotta pay rent."

"Don't we all?"

16.

Ty gets off the bus at 13th and walks the rest of the way to Oscar's office. It looks different in the daylight, the blue paint is peeling in odd places and the front porch is crooked. He steps over the day's paper and rings the doorbell.

"Kid!" Oscar fills the open doorway. "Come on in."

Ty points to the paper. "Don't you want to read that?"

"Human drama," says Oscar, "it's all the same." He shows Ty past the lobby to his dumpy brown desk, motions for him to sit.

"Oscar?"

"Yeah, kid?"

"Did I leave a sack of weed here last week?"

"Nah, kid. I haven't seen any sack of weed. But while you're here, I'll smoke you up." He finds another blunt in the desk drawer, lights it and takes a puff and passes to Ty.

"Thanks."

"No problem, kid. You walk all the way down here?"

"Took the bus." He takes a hit and passes the blunt back.

"How's your friend doing, the one you bailed out?"

"Jackson? Kinda crazy. Been hanging out with that girl he got busted with."

"Not smart," says Oscar. "She's got charges too, and the prosecutor will give her a way out if she offers the right information."

"Bill already told him that."

"She fucking him?"

Ty laughs. "Yeah, she's fucking him."

Oscar takes another hit. "And how about you, kid? How you doing?"

"Trying to make rent next week. Bill got a job."

"You guys married or something?"

"Nah."

"Never can tell these days. So what did you figure out?"

"Huh?"

"To make rent? Did you figure something out?"

"Not really," he says, "but I've still got a week."

They smoke in silence for a while, Oscar's chair squeaking with every movement and Ty still wondering where his sack of weed went. Then Oscar says, "I've got an idea—could help us both out."

Ty takes a hit and smiles. "Yeah?"

"I've got a pick-up this afternoon, some loser who skipped out on his court date. How about you come along with me, like a little extra muscle?"

"Really?" Ty can hardly stay in his seat. "A real pick-up? Handcuffs and everything?"

"Sure, kid. But don't get too excited. He's not exactly Soapy Smith, just some bum who didn't pay child support."

"Who's Soapy Smith?"

"A real boss, back in the day." He stamps the blunt out in the ashtray. "You kids don't know anything these days."

They wait in Oscar's old Buick about half a block down the street from the address handwritten on a scrap of paper.

"How'd you find him?"

"Facebook," says Oscar.

"Facebook?"

"Yeah, I figured out who his girlfriend is and where she works. Followed her back here yesterday. I'm betting our guy shows up."

"Fucking Facebook."

"You kids will put anything on the Internet."

"You think he'll see us, parked out here on the street?"

"Nah, kid. You see, these deadbeats, they're all just lazy know-it-alls. You watch, this guy won't even be paying attention." He pulls a small joint from the glove box and lights it. "Here," he says, "for while we wait."

They smoke and listen to the radio, Oscar telling him a story about Mexico. "My brother owned a nightclub," he says, "an honest business. He even had a mobile DJ van, would go out all over the state to people's weddings, quinceañeras. Then one day, this cartel boss decides he wants a nightclub. Easiest way to do it? Get rid of the competition. So he pays off an inspector and they pull my brother's license."

"Did he fight back, your brother?"

"No, kid. You don't fight back against the cartel. He packed up his family and came to the United States, stayed with us until he got a trucker's license, started running big rigs out to Kansas City and Tulsa."

"And now?"

"Now he owns seven trucks, runs a small shipping company on the north side of town."

"Fuck. I can't even make rent."

"Forget about it, kid. You'll be alright. Do a good job today and I might have some more work for you. My regular guy is hitting the heroin a little too hard lately. He's never around, won't answer my calls. I hate that shit. You come to work for me, you gotta answer my calls."

"Right," says Ty. "Hey—is that him?"

"Where?"

"Coming around the corner, in the yellow Nuggets jersey."

Ty goes to open the door and Oscar stops him. "Easy, kid. Wait 'til he gets up to the front of the apartment building, he'll have fewer directions to run."

So they watch him come around to the front, walking like he doesn't have a care in the world. Then Oscar gets out of the car, walks up quickly behind him, Ty moving around to the side.

The man reaches into his pocket for a set of keys, struggles to find the right one.

"Jacob Baker." Oscar speaks in a deep, commanding voice. "You're under arrest for failure to appear in court. Stay where you are and don't do anything stupid. Now drop those keys to the ground."

Ty watches the man's face go soft, tears forming in his eyes. "Please," says Jacob, "I got a job. I'm trying to catch up on my child support."

Oscar pulls the man's arms behind his back, snaps the handcuffs on. "Just like I told you, kid. A wet noodle."

17.

Tony Giannopoulos sits behind a laminated desk in the back of a run-down payday loan shop out on East Colfax. He taps a shiny leather shoe against the linoleum floor and watches on a flickering monitor as a man walks across the busy store, through the security door into the back office. "Eddie, how'd it go?"

"He don't got the money, Tony."

"Just tell me what happened."

"I walked up to him on the sidewalk, just like you said." Eddie pulls a pack of cigarettes from his shirt pocket. "You mind?"

Tony nods. "Go ahead."

"So anyway, I tell the guy, 'Tony wants his money,' and he just stands there, smiling. Then he says to me, 'Do you know know who I am?' Fucking bum, that's who he is." Eddie takes a drag from his cigarette, flicks the ashes. "He don't got the money, boss."

"Use the ashtray, Eddie—on the desk." Tony leans back in his chair, thinks for a minute. "You sure?"

"Think about it, the guy's wearing cheap pants and doing car commercials. A guy like that gets some money, first thing he's gonna do is buy a new suit."

"But he owns all of those car lots, bought 'em years ago."

"I don't know, Tony. It don't make no sense."

"Fuck it. I'm bringing Elmo up from Texas. He's got a way of finding things that don't want to be found." Tony smiles a little at the thought of his old partner, old times. "Now get me a fucking cigar."

18.

Ty comes crashing through the front door. "Bill! You'll never guess what I did today!" But the living room is empty, the lights are off. He finds Bill in his room, asleep with the shades drawn tight. "Bill! Get up!"

Bill mumbles something and pulls the blanket over his head.

"What? I can't hear you."

"Go away!"

Ty kicks his shoes off and dives onto the bed, jumps around while Bill makes a fuss. Finally, Bill relents. "Okay, what is it?"

"I caught a fugitive." He plops down on the mattress.

"What?" Bill looks confused. He rubs his tired eyes.

"Yeah, a real fugitive—skipped out on his court date."

"How?"

"With Oscar." Ty grins from ear to ear, still high on adrenalin.

"The bail bondsman?"

"I went over there to look for my sack of weed. And we're just talking, smoking, and next thing I know he says, 'Come on, let's make a pick-up.' We waited outside the girlfriend's place for five hours and the guy finally showed up."

"Did you chase him or something?"

"No."

"Slam him down, fight over a weapon?"

"No—it was just some guy who didn't pay his child support. Oscar handcuffed him and we took him to jail."

"Wow," says Bill, "you're a real bounty hunter now, a regular Chapman. This is what you woke me up for?"

"Why do you always have to be such an asshole? Can't you get excited for me, just once?"

"I got excited that time you wore clean socks."

Ty rolls his eyes and tugs at the blanket. "Get up, grumpy. We're going out."

"I worked all day. I'm tired."

"There was a note from Brian under the door. Everyone's going out dancing at Tracks tonight for Patrick's birthday. Put on your cutest outfit and get ready to impress the fabulous gays of Denver."

"Ty, the rent's due next week and we're not even sure we can cover it. I don't think we should be spending our money on booze."

"The boys will buy you drinks." He jumps off the bed. "I didn't tell you the best part! Oscar paid me two hundred dollars for going with him on the pick-up. He says I can do more work next week."

"Two hundred dollars?"

"Yeah, and there's Thai takeout on the kitchen counter."

Bill sits up in bed, sniffs the air and catches the scent of pepper and peanut oil. "I love you like a brother."

"I know," he says. "Just get up already. You're depressing me."

19.

Jackson steps out of the shower, dries his hair with a towel. He walks into the bedroom still naked and plops down on the edge of the bed. "Hey, babe."

"You were in there a long time." She pulls a t-shirt over her head and tugs at the shoulders until it sits the way she likes it.

"I was waiting for you to join me. Aren't you gonna take a shower?"

"Nah, baby. I like your sweat all over me after we've fucked."

"Damn, Vicky. You're crazy."

"And you love it."

"Kinda," he says. "Go roll a joint, and maybe put on some coffee." He follows her out to the living room and watches her start a pot. They sit at an ugly little table and she grinds some bud, rolls a joint.

"Coffee's ready," she says. "You want me to spike it, add a little Kahlua?"

"And set off my ankle monitor? Don't tease me."

She goes to the kitchen counter and comes back with his coffee, a glass of orange juice and a tall shot of vodka for herself. "You gonna smoke all day? We gotta get ready."

"Ready for what?"

"Our big score, dumbass." She gives him a playful look, leans across the table for a kiss. "When we get to Mexico, you can sit around all you want—spend the whole day sleeping and drinking on the beach."

"Mexico? I'm pretty sure they have extradition."

"What does that mean?"

"It means they'll scoop you up and ship you back to the U.S. Marshals."

"Then why do people in the movies always go to Mexico?"

"Just the movies, I guess."

"Okay, so where do we go?"

"Someplace without extradition, like Ecuador or Brazil. Isn't that what the Wikileaks guy did?"

"Is Ecuador warm? I wanna go someplace warm."

"Yeah, babe. It's called Ecuador because it's on the Equator."

"What's that?"

"Never mind. Just pass me the joint." He puts it between his lips and she holds out the lighter. After a few puffs he passes it back and says, "You got any good ideas for the big score? Because I was thinking we could rob someplace at night, drop through the ceiling and hide inside. I heard about this guy up in Westminster—he was robbing car washes by climbing onto the roof and pulling the ladder up behind him. And here's the smart part: This guy, he'd trigger the security alarm and hide up there on the roof. Cops would show up, jiggle the doors a couple times, maybe look in the windows, and think everything was okay. Fucker could take his sweet time loading the money and wiping the place down for prints and shit."

"Don't be stupid," she says. "It's a clever idea, but you gotta hit a lot of places to walk away with a million bucks."

"A million bucks? You think we can get that much?"

"Even a million won't last forever, babe."

She parks the car behind an abandoned warehouse where a chain link fence runs parallel to a set of railroad tracks. A train grinds past, the engine struggling against the weight of its loaded boxcars.

"You sure it's empty?"

She nods. "I used to work here a few years ago when it was a meat packing operation."

"So how do we get inside?"

She pulls a key from her pocket. "I never returned it when I quit the job. Wanna see if it still works?"

They slink through the dark to a rusty metal door on the side of the building. She slides the key into the lock and it opens.

Inside, the only pale light comes from a row of windows, set up high on the southern wall. Various straps and chains and hooks still hang from tracks on the ceiling. Thick spider webs line the corners.

"It's creepy," he says.

"This is where we bring him."

20.

The El Limousine passenger bus rolls to a gentle stop beneath a lighted sign and the automatic door slides open. A crowd, mostly Mexicans coming up from the border towns, spills out of the bus onto the pavement. Men, women, and children gather in small groups around the gravel lot, little piles of belongings kept under close watch. A man with a clipboard is giving directions in Spanish.

Elmo sets his shiny cowboy boot down on the last step, looks around, breathes in the air before stepping off the bus. He carries a small leather bag and wears a white cowboy hat. At the end of the dirty lot he lights a cigarette, turns to face downtown.

A homeless man walks up to him on the sidewalk. "Spare one of those cigarettes, mister?"

Elmo glances at the man then looks down at the pavement, ignores him.

"I said, can you spare a cigarette for a poor soul?"

"Get lost."

The homeless man leans forward, clenches his fingers into tight fists. "What did you say to me?"

"I don't repeat myself."

"That ain't a very nice thing to say, even to a man as low as me." He takes a few steps towards Elmo. "How about I teach you a lesson, stranger?"

Elmo reaches a hand into a pocket, pulls out a small knife and opens it in one smooth movement. "Did you know," he says, "there are dozens of places on the body where even a tiny cut can kill a person?"

The homeless man stops to consider.

"And I know all of them."

"You're crazy," says the man. "All I wanted was a cigarette." He turns and stumbles away, disappears around the corner of the block.

Elmo looks up at the tall buildings, breathes in the heavy fumes of a passing bus. Yeah, he thinks, I hate this city already.

He takes a cab to Tony's office in the back of some shitty little storefront he calls a legitimate business. Even the devil offers better terms.

Inside, there's a girl behind a thick bulletproof window, chewing a wad of gum. "Tell Tony I'm here," he says. "And don't make me wait."

"Tony," she speaks into a little intercom, "some guy's here for you, dressed like a cowboy."

"Elmo!" A door opens and Tony waves him into the back office. "Can I get you anything? How about a stiff drink after such a long bus ride?" He motions to Eddie in the corner. "Get this man a drink."

"Whiskey." Elmo takes a seat. "Why am I here?"

"Don Ulibarri."

"The quarterback? Won the Super Bowl back in—"

Tony interrupts. "Yes, the quarterback. Turns out the asshole's a real bum. He owes me a quarter of a million and won't pay up."

"Why not go after him in court?"

"That's not how I do things." Tony shrugs. "And it's not that kind of loan."

"So you want me to find out why he's not paying?"

Tony nods.

"—and if he doesn't have the money?"

"Then you know what to do."

Elmo exhales deeply, brings his hands to his chin and thinks. "I want twenty percent." He lets the number hang for a moment. "You get your money, I get fifty grand for the trouble."

Tony smiles. "Ten percent."

"Twenty," says Elmo. "I don't negotiate—you know that. Now let's say your guy doesn't have the money and you want me to kill the fucker and do it clean, without no evidence—that's another fifty."

Tony looks over to Eddie, still standing by the door. "You see? Don Ulibarri, the great quarterback, you see what this guy does to me?" He shakes his head and waves a hand at Elmo. "Make it happen."

Elmo leaves the office and Tony lights a cigar. Eddie finds a bottle of brandy and pours them each a drink. "You trust this cowboy?"

"He ain't a real cowboy, just dresses like one."

"He gives me the creeps."

"Elmo? He's alright. I know him from El Paso, back when I had the pawn shops. Did some work for me then, too. Real useful guy, that Elmo. Doesn't ask too many questions—like he enjoys it or something."

"Enjoys what?"

"Hurting people."

21.

Oscar's car smells like hot dogs. He and Ty eat footlongs and drink sodas while they wait for another bail jumper. "Not too fast, kid. You drink too much and you'll have to take a leak in the car. We're not going anywhere for a while."

Ty wipes mustard from his lip. "I can't believe you put ketchup on your hot dog. That's just wrong, Oscar. In some places you can get killed for that."

"Just be quiet and eat, maybe learn something." He sucks soda through a straw. "Listen, this case, it's different than the last one. This guy's edgy, might try to run off or put up a fight."

"How do you know?"

"You been doing this as long as I have, you just know. The dumbass did time for stealing a car and giving the cops a good chase. He's looking at prison on this one. No family. Nothing to lose. You see the pattern."

"Do I get a gun?"

"No! You don't get a gun, and you keep asking questions like that, I'll drive you right back to the office. This is business, kid, not a videogame." He lights a cigarette, takes a drag. "You know what happens to heroes?"

Ty shakes his head.

"They die young—little soldiers marching off to fight a war, or newly-minted gangsters in search of a fast buck. And there's always another hero, ready to take the last one's place." He leans forward, cranks the driver-side window open. "I don't need you to be a hero, Ty. I need you to be smart. That's how we get what we want."

Ty thinks about what Oscar said. "Can I have a cigarette?"

"I thought you didn't smoke these filthy things."

"Just one," says Ty, "with you."

Oscar smiles and hands him the pack of smokes. "This job, it's like anything else worth doing. We gotta be creative, outsmart the other guy."

Ty nods and lights his cigarette.

"Let me ask you something? Suppose you want to get back at someone who hurt you real bad. Let's say he killed your sister."

"I don't have a sister."

"Just go along with it. Now let's say this guy is bigger than you, badder than you, and everyone knows how tough he is."

"I follow." Ty cranks down his window, blows smoke through the crack.

"Now you're the one going after the guy. What do you do? Send him a message? Tell him you're coming?" Oscar slams his fists down hard against the steering wheel. "No! You creep into his house under the cover of darkness and slit his throat while he sleeps. Maybe you shoot the poor fucker in the dick while he's pinching a loaf. That's how you do it."

"Stack the odds in your favor?"

"Yes!" says Oscar. "Now you get it." He lights another cigarette. "We catch 'em by surprise, take 'em when they least expect it."

Ty grins. "How'd you get so smart, Oscar?"

"I paid for it with a lot of dumb mistakes. Now smoke your cigarette, kid, and shut the fuck up."

An hour later his bladder is burning. "Oscar," he says, "I have to pee."

"You've got your cup. Fill it."

"Here? Next to you?"

"Go ahead. I won't look."

Ty turns to face away from Oscar, cracks the door and pours the rest of his lukewarm soda on the pavement, puts the empty cup between his legs.

"You peeing yet?"

"I can't do it with you talking."

"Alright. Relax." Oscar goes to light another cigarette, brings the lighter up to his mouth and stops short. "That's our guy!"

"Where?"

"At the end of the block, coming out of the convenience store."

"Fuck! Now I'm peeing!"

"Well cut it off!"

"Once I start peeing I can't stop. And you're making me nervous—not helping the cause, man."

"Helping the what? Hurry, he's got his hands full with bags. Now's the time."

"I'm done! I'm done! No—I'm not done!"

"Fuck, kid! He's coming towards us." Oscar lowers his voice. "Crouch down. That's it, get low. You finished yet or what?"

"Yeah, but my hands are all—"

"Shhh!"

They crouch down low in the old Buick and watch their mark walk down the sidewalk, a plastic grocery bag in each hand.

"Wait a couple seconds," says Oscar, "come up from behind." Then he opens the door and goes left around the backside of the car. "Josiah Hernández," he says in a deep voice, "you're under arrest for failure to appear in Denver County Court."

"Fuck!" Josiah pivots on his heels, drops the bags and coils up to take off running.

Oscar reaches for him. Too late. "Grab him, Ty!"

Ty opens the door and steps out into the running man's path. They collide and go down in a pile of swinging arms and legs. A hard blow lands on Ty's chin. He's stunned for a moment but the shock turns to anger and he fights back. "You're under arrest!"

Oscar lands a knee on Josiah's back and comes out with a pair of handcuffs. First he gets one wrist, then the other.

They load their catch into the backseat and Oscar gets in next to him. "You're driving, kid."

"But I don't have a license."

"You know where the jail is?"

"Yeah."

"Then fuck it—let's go."

His hands shake all the way to the jail. Oscar surrenders their prize to a plain-faced deputy—a stark figure in a neatly ironed shirt—and climbs back into the passenger seat. "How you doing, kid? How's the face?"

"Hurts like hell."

"It'll be sore a few days but you'll live." He takes another cigarette from his shirt pocket, hands one over to Ty. "You gonna play this game, you gotta take your hits."

Ty smiles.

"Come on, kid. Let's go for milkshakes."

22.

The house is empty. Don left an hour ago in a white BMW sport utility; Elmo watched him blow through a stop sign on his way out of the neighborhood.

It'll be easy, he thinks. Wait for him to get back from the bar—guys like Don are always reliving their legend at a local sports bar—and knock him out in the driveway. There's a room prepared in the back of one of Tony's storefronts. It won't take much to get the truth.

Then he sees a shadow, a figure moving in the dark, disappear silently behind the corner of Don Ulibarri's garage. Elmo dials Tony and waits while the phone rings.

"Hello?" Tony sounds drunk.

"Are you making a move?"

"What—what the fuck are you talking about?"

"Someone else is here."

"Who?"

"The fuck if I know. I just watched them go behind Don Ulibarri's garage."

There's the sound of an approaching engine. A pair of headlights swing onto the road behind him, beams reflected in the side mirror. "Hold on." He drops the phone onto the passenger seat and ducks down, watches Don pass in his BMW, the SUV turning into the driveway and the garage door opening. In the light of the garage, Elmo sees

Don get out of the car, the figure dressed in black creeping in from the dark. "Holy shit."

"What the fuck is going on over there?" Tony Giannopoulos is screaming on the other end of the phone. Elmo ignores him, opens the glove box and grabs a pair of binoculars for a closer look.

The man dressed in black carries a metal bat wrapped up in rags and duct tape. He swings it hard at the back of Don's head and the big man goes down, a pile of drunken flesh on the concrete floor.

A second car turns onto the street—a rusty Subaru. It pulls into the driveway behind Don's BMW and another figure in black gets out. They work together, dragging the dead weight to the back of the car, lifting it up and into the trunk. Then they're backing out of the driveway, tires screeching, blowing the same damn stop sign on the way out of the neighborhood. Elmo scribbles the plate number on a burger wrapper.

Tony's still shouting on the other end of the line. Elmo picks up the phone, puts it to his ear and winces at the sound of Tony's voice. "Listen," he says, "there's a problem."

23.

She takes the corner hard, tires squeal on dark asphalt. Jackson steadies himself in the passenger seat, his heart pounding away. "Don't speed! That's how they always get caught. Ain't you never seen COPS?"

"You sure he's knocked out?"

"I cracked that fucker good." He laughs, a crazy burst of energy. "Whack! Right in the back of the head."

"I thought you might have killed him."

"Maybe if I swung a little harder." He bounces in the seat. "Fuck!" he shouts. "I can't believe we did it!"

"Easy, babe. We're just getting started." She puts a cigarette between her lips, Newport 100's from the green box, and he lights it for her. "I think you're right, you know?" The car slows a little.

"About what?" He scratches the side of his head.

"We gotta play it smart, stay cool and avoid unnecessary attention. The last thing we need is some nosy traffic cop blowing everything."

"Yeah, babe. Now give me one of those cigarettes."

They pull up to the abandoned meat packing warehouse and Jackson gets out with the baseball bat. When he gives the signal, she lifts the trunk lid and steps back.

"I think he's still out." He laughs again. "Damn, I cracked him good."

"You sure? What if he's faking?"

He pokes their limp victim with the baseball bat. "See," he says, "out like a light bulb."

In a blur of polyester and flabby flesh the old quarterback lunges up from the floor of the trunk, roars like a beast and grabs tight around Jackson's neck. Jackson swings the bat into the quarterback's head, but the big man doesn't go down. He swings again. And again. "Fuck you!" he screams. "Dumb fucking jock! Fuck you!" Blood splatters onto his shirt and neck and face and then the man is still again.

"Damn," says Vicky, "he's a monster."

"Yeah, now help me drag him."

24.

Elmo stands in the doorway of Tony's office. Tony is in a mad rage like back in the old El Paso days.

"I don't understand how this happened!"

"What's there to understand?" says Elmo. "He got jumped in his garage, hauled away in the trunk of a car."

"I heard you the first time. But why the very same night I send you after him?"

"This quarterback Ulibarri, he sounds like a real bum. Probably owes money all over town."

"You think they saw you?"

"Who? The kidnappers?" Elmo lights a cigarette. "Nah, they didn't see me—just blew right past me burnin' rubber all the way. The whole thing looked a bit amateur if you want my professional opinion."

"You get a look at 'em?" Tony takes a cigarette from the pack on his desk, Eddie steps in from his usual place in the corner to offer a lighter.

"They covered their faces—at least they weren't that stupid."

"You're not helping."

"I got the license plate number." Elmo smiles. "447-FRX."

Tony takes two shot glasses from a drawer, fills them from a bottle of tequila and slides one over to Elmo. "That's why I like you, Texan.

Got a good head on your shoulders." He lifts his glass in the air, drinks it in one easy gulp. "Find them."

"My time is expensive."

"Of course, because you're known for the expediency of your work." Tony pours himself another shot and drops it down his open throat. "I've got a friend inside the police department. You give that license plate number to Eddie and we'll get you an address, something to go on."

"There's a chance the car is boosted—could be abandoned somewhere, wiped down for prints or set on fire."

"You said they're amateurs." Tony takes a drink straight from the bottle, runs a hand through a greasy mop of hair. "Amateurs always make mistakes."

25.

They sit in a tall booth at the front of the diner, looking out through a huge window at Colfax Boulevard and the day drinkers and the busy traffic of the city. The waitress comes by with a second round of coffee. She touches Ty on the arm. "Your pancakes are on the griddle."

"Thanks," he says.

"Maple syrup?" She raises an eyebrow. Her face is young and framed by messy brown hair.

"Please, and extra butter."

"Sure thing." She goes off to another table. They watch her pour coffee and make small talk with the patrons.

"She likes you, kid."

Ty blushes. "Nah, she's just being friendly."

Oscar laughs. "I come here fifteen years and ain't none of the waitresses ever been so nice to me. Not even the ugly ones."

"That's because you're a crappy tipper."

"Yeah, maybe. How's your face?"

"Still a little sore, getting better."

Oscar takes a bite of his pie. "You really handled yourself out there, kid. It wasn't the strongest showing, but you weren't afraid to jump in and get your hands dirty." He puts a small white box on the table. "For you."

"Oscar, you didn't have to—"

"Open it."

Ty takes the box in both hands, holds it in front of him like a treasure. He lifts the lid, peeks inside and sees shiny metal—a pair of handcuffs.

"Look closely, I had them engraved with your initials."

"I—I don't know what to say. I'm honored." He lifts the handcuffs from the box, turns them around in his hands and feels the weight.

The waitress sets a steaming stack of pancakes down in front of him. "You guys planning something kinky?"

"It's not—"

"Hey, I don't judge."

"He's a bail bondsman," says Oscar. "My new assistant."

"Impressive." She puts a hand out towards Ty. "I'm Dylan. What's your name?"

He wipes his sweaty palm on his shorts, reaches out to shake her hand. "Ty."

Oscar interrupts. "Dylan? Isn't that a boy's name?"

"Do I look like a boy?"

"Not like any boy I've seen."

"Then maybe you haven't been going to the right parties." She rests her elbow on Ty's shoulder. "You got a number? You know, in case I need to get bailed out or something."

"I don't have a phone—I mean, I have a phone, but it got shut off."

"Oh."

"Wait a minute." Oscar slides a new iPhone across the table. "Got it activated this morning."

"Oscar!" Ty grins wide.

"My new assistant ain't no good to me without a phone. Now go ahead and get her number."

26.

Don Ulibarri's head never hurt so fucking bad, not even the time he got carried off the field during a playoff game. His wrists are bound behind him with duct tape and a thick chain is padlocked around his ankles—the other end locked to a metal support column. There's the smell of old meat left to rot, the smell of death.

He tries to scream and hears only a muffled groan, the sound caught in his throat. A rag covers his mouth, held tight with more tape. He screams again, and again, and is sure he can't breathe, then everything goes dark.

Two voices, coming from the hall: "He's not worth anything to us if he dies."

"They'd pay—for the body—for a proper burial."

Then it's black again.

27.

Bill's feet ache. He's been standing on the sales floor for five and a half hours, his only break a quick fifteen minutes.

"Fatal Vengeance?"

"Huh?"

"Do you have Fatal Vengeance, the video game?" A large woman with a demanding voice stands in front of him with her hands on her hips.

"I'm not sure, ma'am. I'll help you look."

"The website says you have it." Her face is stern. "I looked before I got in the car."

He shows her over to a row of displays. "Tell me the name again."

"Fatal Vengeance." She checks her phone and looks around. "Does anyone competent work here?"

Anger. The feeling is anger rising up in his chest. He takes a breath, thinks of smoking a fat bowl after work. "Why don't we search through the inventory on the computer?"

She follows him over to the service kiosk and watches him type the game's title into the search field. A spinning icon. The results: 0 units in store.

"You better do something about this."

"I'm sorry, ma'am. We're out of that game."

"You can't be out; the website says you have it."

"It's possible someone bought it. When did you check?"

She uncrosses her arms, points an accusing finger at him. "Oh, so you're saying I'm wrong? How can I be wrong? I'm the customer."

"It's not really a moral question, ma'am. Right or wrong, we don't have a copy of that game." He points to the screen. "There's a copy at Park Meadows."

"How dare you?" She takes a wide stance. "Get your manager."

He presses a button and speaks into the little walkie-talkie. They wait in awkward silence, then a manager in a white shirt appears, walking quickly between the rows of shelves.

"I'm Steve. How can I help you?"

"Your website says you have this game in stock, and now your employee is telling me you don't have it." She sends a text on her phone while talking.

"Yes, well sometimes there's a delay on the website."

She doesn't look up. "That's not my problem. It's yours. I'm not going anywhere until I get that game."

"I'm sorry, but we don't have it. I can order a copy for you, have it shipped to the store or your residence at no extra charge."

"It's my son's birthday today. He's turning eleven, and all he wants for his birthday is Fatal Vengeance."

"I'm really sorry, ma'am. Sometimes these things happen."

"Well that's not good enough." She points to Bill. "And this guy gave me attitude, tried to tell me I'm wrong."

Bill interrupts. "That's not what I said, ma'am."

"See!" She jabs her pointed finger. "He's doing it again! Giving me attitude, when you're the one who ruined my son's birthday. He's never going to get over this."

Bill can't take it any longer. The woman's self-righteousness, the apathetic manager, the scratchy blue shirt—it's all too humiliating, too degrading for him. "If it's so important why'd you wait until the last minute to buy his gift?"

"See how he talks to me, a paying customer!"

"You haven't paid for anything."

The manager waves him off. "On behalf of the company, I apologize. I can offer you a gift card to help make things right."

"Fire that employee. That would make things right."

"Customer service is always our number one priority. His behavior will be addressed according to company policy."

She thinks over the manager's offer, twists her lips into a little knot. "How much is the gift card?"

He's taking his last break, drinking shitty coffee at a wobbly table. The manager walks in, pours himself a cup and takes a seat.

"You firing me?"

"Written warning," says the manager. "Besides, that woman is a total fucking bitch."

28.

The tiny camera shop on South Broadway doesn't do much business these days. Harry thinks it's because all the kids are buying online, going digital. Who needs film when you've got Photoshop?

The phone rings. He recognizes the number. "Hello?"

"Hey, Harry. It's Tom."

"Hey, Tom."

"I can't make it in this afternoon. My doctor's appointment at the VA got pushed back and they won't see me until four."

"Okay, Tom. Just take care." Another double shift, he thinks. Better call Nancy and tell her I'll be late for dinner.

The little bell above the door announces a customer. He watches him enter, a young guy in baggy clothes with some kind of device strapped to one of his ankles. Must be what the kids are wearing these days. "Hey there, fella," he says. "What can I help you with?"

"I'm looking for a video camera."

"What are you planning to use it for?"

"Does it matter?"

"Well, sure. You tell me what you're planning on getting up to, and I can recommend the right equipment for the job."

"Okay," says the young man. "I'm interviewing someone."

"Oh, I got all kinds of gear for that. You gonna be indoors or outdoors?"

"Why?"

"The lighting is different, for starters."

"Indoors, I guess." He glances around the shop, looks over his shoulder to the front door. "You got something simple to use?"

Harry senses the man's uneasiness. "Sounds like you just need a flipcam—something point and shoot you can plug into a computer, upload to your YouTube channel."

"Or email?"

"Huh?"

"Could I email the videos?"

"Well, sure. It's as simple as attaching the file, as long as it's not too big."

The man asks to see one. Harry shows him an entry-level model, hands it over so he can take a closer look. "Now that one there's got the microphone built right in, records video and sound. $199 includes the USB cord."

"And the batteries? I hate when it doesn't include the batteries."

"Oh yes, rechargeable batteries included." Harry looks down at the man's shoes, scratches his head. "Say, young man, what's that on your ankle?"

The man sticks his foot out in front of him. "Alcohol monitoring bracelet. Court-ordered, as part of my pre-trial release."

"Looks uncomfortable."

"It's tight and itches like hell."

Harry says, "You mind if I ask what you did?"

"Just acting stupid. Got a second DUI, cocaine in the car." He laughs.

"You think it's funny?"

"Which part?"

"All of it." There's a moment of silence between them; Harry's back muscles tense. "Well anyway, it's $199 if you want the camera, plus tax."

"But I don't got $199. Besides, I only need it once."

"Well, if you don't have the money you can't buy the camera." He holds out an open hand. "Now give it back."

"I don't like the way you're talking to me. What if I just take it?" The young man grabs the box and USB cord from the display counter. "I don't see no security cameras."

Harry grimaces. He remembers his wife telling him to install a surveillance system, but he always felt it made a place seem cold, impersonal. "Take it," he says. "Just get out of my store."

The delinquent stares back at him, let's the moment hang before he turns around, walks out casually through the front door. The little bell dings.

Harry doesn't move. He waits to be sure the man with the ankle bracelet is gone, then he takes a deep breath, steadies himself against the edge of the display counter. First a double shift, he thinks, and now I get robbed. What's next? I'm not telling Nancy about this, no way. She's always saying that I'm wrong, that people aren't good anymore.

He scratches his head. I don't know, he thinks, maybe she's right.

29.

"You know why I like this place?" Tony waves a syrupy fork over a stack of pancakes. "Look around. It's old fashioned. The waitresses still smell like cheap hairspray and cigarettes, call you 'honey.' None of that corporate bullshit taking the life out of everything it touches like that guy, you know—"

"Who?"

"Oh, come on, Elmo." Tony snaps his fingers. "You know, that guy, turns everything he touches into stone."

"You mean Medusa?"

"No, dummy. Medusa was the eyes. This guy touches you." He drops his fork to the plate. "Oh, never mind. I've got the report back on the Subaru."

"And?"

"Car belongs to some dildo named Mark Lipinski, lives over in South Aurora."

"You know the guy?"

"Never fucking heard of him." Tony goes back to eating his pancakes.

Elmo rubs his chin, motions to the waitress for another cup of coffee. "Was it reported stolen?"

"Huh?"

"The car, was it reported stolen?"

"Nope."

"Something about this don't make no sense."

"That's what I've been saying."

"I'm serious," says Elmo. "The car—some random guy from the suburbs—it's not adding up right." He takes a sip of coffee, lightly taps his fingers against the tabletop. "There's something we're missing."

A thin line of syrup runs down Tony's chin. "That's what I'm paying you to figure out."

30.

It's a bland suburb, like any other—the same corporate restaurants serving overweight rubes, the same fast-food, the same stores and cars and people. Elmo turns into the neighborhood, flicks his cigarette out of the window and lights another. He parks a couple doors down, watches the house.

Daylight turns to dusk. The lights are on in the house, signs of movement. A blue Toyota Prius pulls into the garage and the door closes behind it. Elmo pisses into an empty 7/11 cup and lights the last cigarette of the pack. He groans when he gets out of the car. I'm getting too old, he thinks. This is young man shit.

The doorbell is a pleasant two-tone chime. A woman wearing a cooking apron answers. "Hello? Can I help you?"

"Is Mark Lipinski home?"

"Do you know him? May I ask your business?"

"Well, ma'am, I'm a detective with the Aurora Police Department."

A man steps into the open doorway behind the woman. "What's going on here? Can't you see the sign?" He points to a red 'No Soliciting' decal on the door.

"Honey, this man is a police detective."

"Mark Lipinski?" Elmo flashes a badge and official-looking ID. "I have some questions regarding a red Subaru that's registered in your name."

"Damnit, Vicky." Mark Lipinski tells his wife to go inside, steps onto the stoop and closes the door. "What did that girl do now?"

"How do you mean?"

"My daughter, Vicky. I bought the Subaru for her and it's been nothing but trouble. Two accidents and a stack of speeding tickets. My insurance tripled."

"I see."

"She's not dead, is she?"

"No, Mr. Lipinski, she's not dead."

"Then what did she do?"

"Sir?"

"Why are you looking for her?"

"I'm afraid it's rather serious," says Elmo. "Vicky may have witnessed a violent crime and I'm looking for answers."

Mark sighs, lets out a nervous chuckle. "I'm kinda relieved. When you flashed that badge I thought you were coming to arrest her." He pauses. "Vicky's always been a handful. Truth is, we're pretty worried about her."

"Why's that?"

"She's a good girl, officer. She really is. But Vicky likes to fall in with the wrong crowd. Normal life—working and making a living—doesn't hold much interest for her."

Like half the girls from the suburbs, Elmo thinks. The other half keep busy outdoing their mothers. "When's the last time you saw her, Mr. Lipinski?"

"Shit, been at least a couple of months, but she calls here and there and I put up some bail money a few weeks back. Gave her money for rent, too."

"Any idea where she's staying?"

"Last we heard she rents a place in the city, but she won't give us the address. It's like I said officer, Vicky's not a bad person—"

The door opens behind him. Mrs. Lipinski is wringing her hands. "Does he want to arrest her, the police officer?"

"He just wants to ask her some questions, honey. Go back inside."

"I know who she's dating," she says. "Maybe it'll help."

"Yes, ma'am." Elmo feigns concern. "Why don't you step out here and fill me in?"

She steps into the cool evening air, pulls a light sweater tightly around her shoulders. "I just want to know if she's safe. Will you call and tell us if you find her?"

"Of course."

"Sometimes," says Mrs. Lipinski, "I check Vicky's Instagram profile."

"Instagram?"

"It's an app."

Elmo shrugs his shoulders.

"People share pictures, photo updates with their friends." She unlocks her phone and taps the screen. "Here's Vicky's account."

Elmo takes his first look at the girl. She's drunk, holding a beer in one hand and a cigarette in the other. She wears a bikini top with cut-off jean shorts and a silly cowboy hat. They scroll through more photos; more partying, more booze, more bikinis.

"She likes to have fun," says Mrs. Lipinski. "Here. The guy's name is Small. They're in some pictures together."

Elmo sees a big man in the photo, wearing a black 'SECURITY' t-shirt over a pair of designer jeans. Vicky leans against his thick bicep and shoulder, wraps her arms around his neck.

"He's a bouncer," she says, "at a club."

"You know which one"?

"Bar Standard. It's on Lincoln, in the city."

"You've been most helpful, Mrs. Lipinski."

"Remember," Mrs. Lipinski speaks in nervous bursts, "if you find her—"

"You'll be the first to know." Elmo turns to Mr. Lipinski. "If you don't mind my asking, what do you do?"

"For a living?"

"Yes, sir."

"I sell carpet."

"Thank you, Mr. Lipinski. I'll look you up next time I need a rug."

Elmo goes back to the car, rummages around for a cigarette before he realizes they're all gone. He stops at a little Korean market on Havana for a fresh pack and a gets a shitty cup of coffee. Serves me right, he thinks. What the fuck do Koreans know about coffee?

He lights a smoke and opens the glove box, grabs a prepaid phone and makes a call.

"Hello?"

"Who's this?"

"No, you first. Who the fuck is this?"

"It's me. Elmo."

"Fucking Christ, Elmo. What's going on out there? I've been trying to reach you for hours."

"I left the phone in the glove box."

"What the fuck? I give you a phone, that means you're supposed to carry it. That's the whole point of me giving you a fucking phone."

"I never did care for technology."

"Fuck what you like. Did you find our guy?"

"It's not him."

"What do you mean it's not him?"

"Mark Lipinski sells carpet and drives a Prius. He's harmless. Now the daughter, she's a bit of a wild one."

"The daughter? You think she had something to do with this?"

Elmo takes a long drag, makes Tony wait. "She drives the car," he says, "and the folks ain't seen her for months."

"Alright, it's something to go on. Now get your ass back here. I need you to go with Eddie on a run."

"You're paying me, right? I guess that makes you the boss."

31.

It's another one of Tony's payday loan shops, this time on Federal, the signs all painted on the windows in Spanish. Tony shows Elmo around, boasts about how good the shop is doing. "My top performer," he says. "Reminds me of El Paso, all the fucking Mexicans I used to hire to work the counter. Say what you will about Mexicans, but those people can hustle."

"Maybe that's the problem with white folks," says Elmo.

"How do you mean?"

"We lost our hustle." Elmo looks around the lobby. There's a woman with two small children, waiting patiently for her number to be called. A neon sign flickers in the window. "How late do you stay open?"

"Twenty-four hours. Got myself an armed guard to keep the peace—late night crowd gets rowdy."

"You're telling me people walk in that late looking for a payday loan?"

"Shit, yeah. The most desperate ones, too. Got 'em bent over a fucking barrel with my interest rates." He laughs. "You wanna know the best part?"

"You gonna tell me, or build up for dramatic effect?"

"Don't be smart." He leads Elmo through a side door into the back office. "In a few years I'm out. Gonna sell everything and retire and take my wife down to Belize. You ever been to Belize?"

Elmo shakes his head from side to side.

"We went down there last year—beautiful—you should see the fucking beaches. And it's English-speaking. None of that Spanish jibber jabber. Heard they even have a law to keep the homos out. What was I saying? Oh yes, I'm gonna sell the whole thing, Elmo. Sixteen shops. I'm cashing out."

"And the drug deals you've been financing? The loans made off the books?"

"The icing on the cake, my friend."

"I hate icing. Too sweet."

'Tony leans back in his chair. "Listen, I need you to go on a run with Eddie tonight—show him how we did things back in El Paso. Like old times."

"What's the job?"

"The usual, some guy who owes me money. Only this guy can't pay. I know because it's the fifth loan I've made to the sorry bastard. They say you can't squeeze blood from a stone, but I've been squeezing this guy pretty good."

"Killing someone is extra."

"Did I say I want him dead?" Tony lights a cigar, rolls it around between his lips.

"Oh," says Elmo, "I just assumed."

Elmo rides shotgun, watches Eddie drive. "You been working for Tony long?"

"Five years. My wife is Tony's sister. She didn't give me much of a choice, if you know what I mean."

Elmo snorts. "I don't know. I ain't never been married."

"You're better off. All I get from that woman is trouble. But my two girls are little angels. She gave me that." Eddie takes a pack of Marlboro cigarettes from his shirt pocket, offers one to Elmo. "You must have a lot of stories about Tony, huh? From El Paso, back in the day?"

"Nothing too interesting."

"Oh, come on. All those pawn shops? Tony says you guys did anything for a buck, even ran wetbacks across the border—lost a few in the back of a hot truck."

Elmo smiles. "Whatever we did, I ain't saying. 1361 Yosemite, this is it."

Eddie pulls the car up to the curb, parks behind a white utility van and shuts off the engine. He goes to open the door and Elmo stops him. "We wait," says Elmo, "watch the building for a while, get a feel for who's around."

"Right. You want another cigarette?"

An hour passes. They sit in the car and smoke. Elmo cracks the window and listens to cars pass, watches the light of the TV flickering in the deadbeat's apartment. Eddie dozes in the passenger seat until Elmo nudges him awake.

They cross the street to the front of the building and make their way up a narrow staircase to the apartment. Elmo stands to the side of the door and tells Eddie to knock.

"What should I say?"

"I don't know. Just tell him it's the manager."

"Do I look like the fucking manager?"

"Just knock already. Let's go."

Eddie knocks and they hear someone inside, footsteps crossing the room to the door. "Who is it?"

"The manager."

"Rent isn't due until next week, so what do you want?"

Eddie looks at Elmo, hesitates. "Uh, there's a problem with the building's water. We're going into each apartment."

The door cracks open. "It's late."

"Yeah, we're real sorry about that."

Elmo slams his weight into the door, the force of it knocking the man on the other side down to the floor. He's on top of him in seconds, puts a knife to his throat.

The man starts to cry. His body is skeletal, his face like wrinkled tissue paper.

"What's your name, son?"

"Dominic. My name is Dominic."

"All you gotta do, Dominic, is stop that crying and come with us. You walk out to the car real nicely and I'll put the knife back in my pocket.

Dominic nods and dries his eyes. "Can I get a shirt?"

Elmo shakes his head. "Where we're going you won't need one."

Eddie drives. Elmo's in the backseat with Dominic, who's got a bad case of the shakes. "What—what do you want from me?"

"What we want," says Elmo, "is Tony Giannopoulos' money. But it's a little late for that."

"I can get it—the money."

"We both know that isn't true. Easy now, you keep shaking like that and you're gonna piss yourself. And you better not piss in Tony's car."

They cross railroad tracks and turn into a dark alley. Eddie shuts off the engine and Elmo asks for one of Tony's cigars. He lights it and takes a few quick puffs until the end is glowing hot. "Tony sure does like his cigars. You like cigars, Dominic?"

"Yeah—I guess so."

"Well you must, Dominic. Because when you don't pay Mr. Giannopoulos, it's like snatching the cigar right outta his mouth. What do you think Mr. Giannopoulos would do if you snatched the cigar outta his mouth?"

"I don't know."

Elmo leans his weight into Dominic, smashes him into the door panel. He brings the cigar around with his left hand, presses it deep and hard into the soft skin on the ragged man's neck. "You like that? You fucking like that?" He opens the door, kicks Dominic—trembling and screaming and grabbing at his neck—into the dirty alley.

"Please, I didn't mean to. I'm sorry. I'm fucking sorry."

Elmo kicks him in the ribs, once, twice. "Come on, Eddie, help me turn him on his other side."

They roll him over, still kicking and screaming, and Eddie pins him to the ground. Elmo comes in with the cigar again, presses it into the other side of Dominic's neck until he wails and begs for mercy. Somewhere nearby a dog is barking.

"You tell anyone about tonight, about Tony, and I'll fucking kill you myself. You fucking hear me?"

Dominic nods. "Okay—anything—just please don't kill me." A dark wet patch appears over his crotch.

"Now you did it," says Elmo, "went and pissed your pants." He jumps forward, kicks Dominic hard in the face. Dominic brings his arms and hands up in front of him, tries to block the assault, but Elmo keeps kicking. Blood pours from the beaten man's mouth and nose.

"Motherfucker! Fucking deadbeat piece of shit white trash!" Elmo kicks and kicks and kicks. "I'll kill you! I'll fucking kill you!"

Eddie takes a few steps back, avoids the splatter of blood. "He's had enough, Elmo. Fuck."

A bloody tooth falls out of Dominic's mouth, then another.

They take his wallet and leave him there, a limp pile of human flesh in the red glow of their taillights. Then Elmo wipes the blood from his face, turns to Eddie. "You wanna go for milkshakes?" He smiles, a big devilish smile. "My treat."

They're sitting in the parking lot, Eddie sucking on a chocolate shake and Elmo having his vanilla.

"Elmo?" Eddie's tone is cautious. "How do you do it?"

"Do what?"

"Beat a person like that, almost to death?"

"I don't know." Elmo picks the cherry out of his shake. "I stopped caring a long time ago."

32.

They prop Don up against the wall, rip the tape from his mouth. He spits and gags and takes a few deep breaths. His hands are taped up behind him, his legs still chained to a support column. There's an open sore on his ankle where the padlock rubs, and he's been shitting into a bucket for three days.

"So all you do is press here?" She points to a silver button on the side of the camera. "And it records?"

"Pretty sure," says Jackson. "The old man showed me—before I robbed him." He lets out a little laugh. "But don't talk when we're recording. The cops got voice identification and shit."

"Duh, babe. Do I look stupid?"

"Just saying. You got the script?"

She goes to another room and comes back with a single piece of paper, a few sentences scribbled on it with permanent marker.

Jackson holds it up for Don. "Can you read this?"

Don's expression doesn't change.

"Look fucker, I'll beat you senseless again. Maybe even kill you."

"No, you won't."

"Why the fuck not?" Jackson pulls back his shoulders, puffs out his chest and breathes through his nostrils.

Don nods at Vicky. "Because she won't let you."

Jackson curls his hand into a fist. "I'm warning you douchebag. You keep talking shit like that—"

"Focus," says Vicky. "The video ain't gonna record itself."

Don laughs. "Is this where you record me saying that if my people don't send the ransom money you'll cut off a finger, maybe an ear?"

"Shut up and read what we tell you to read."

"Let's see it."

Jackson holds the paper out. Vicky tells Don to start reading then hits record on the camera.

"My name is Don Ulibarri, Super Bowl Champion and owner—for fuck's sake they know who I am." He regroups, continues reading. "I have been kidnapped by professionals from Mexico City. The choice is simple, pay one million dollars or bury my dead body." He stops reading, laughs until the laughing turns into heavy coughing.

"You think this is funny, motherfucker?"

Vicky stops recording. "Damnit, Jackson. You talked while it was going."

"It's okay. We can't use that anyway."

Don's face is flush and a thin strip of mucus hangs from his chin. "The two of you—like Bonnie and Clyde. Do you know what happened to them?"

"Who the fuck are Bonnie and Clyde?"

"Just a couple of petty robbers who died in a hail of gunfire."

"We're not petty robbers."

"Oh, right," says Don, "you're kidnapping professionals from Mexico City. Now I suggest you drop me off at a hospital before things get worse."

"You're the one tied up, motherfucker." Jackson grabs his crotch. "Now do what we say or I'll break your fucking jaw."

"You think you'd be the first?" Don spits—a big phlegmy wad. "Here's the thing—you ain't getting a fucking penny, 'cause there ain't no money to get."

Vicky glances sideways at Jackson, a worried look. "What do you mean, there ain't no money?"

"I'm broke—hell, bankrupt." He spits again, chuckles. "They're coming for the house any day now."

"No—" Her face goes flat.

"Yes," he says. "You idiots kidnapped a worthless fuck."

Vicky twists her lower lip between her fingers. "But the car dealerships—sixteen dealerships—your name on the sign."

"And none of it's mine." He drops his head, rocks it side to side and stretches his neck muscles. "I sold all of my dealerships to a group of investors. Shit, it's been almost a decade."

"But you're on TV."

"Those shitty commercials? Oh, they pay me. Money goes straight to my ex-wife in the form of child support and alimony. $8,000 a month. You believe that shit? What kind of bitch needs $8,000 a month?"

"Fuck!" Vicky paces in the tiny office, scratches at her face.

Jackson slams his fist into the wall. "He's lying. Gotta be. Look at him—fucking liar. He's just telling us that so we'll let him go."

"We're not letting him go," she says. "No fucking way. We'll kill him if we have to—figure out a way to collect the insurance money or something."

For the first time in a while Don is smiling.

33.

"Bill—" Another manager in a white shirt. "We're going to need you on parking lot duty. Hurry up and get out there."

"I was under the impression that my role is in customer service."

"Your job description says you will perform any task requested by the company, including those beyond your regular duties."

"Would I have to take a bullet for the CEO?"

"Don't be smart, Bill. Grab a safety vest and get to work."

Carts are flung to the farthest reaches of the parking lot. He finds one tossed on its side in a rocky drainage ditch. Who does that? He wonders if people are even worth saving—as if by some some means he could save them.

With a bit of doing he gets a column of carts strung together and pushes them towards the front of the store. The bright, Colorado sun beats down on the black asphalt and he sweats. He passes a mom loading her daughter into a gold SUV.

"Do you want me to take that back?"

The daughter screams, "No!"

"I will! I'll march it right back into the store. Just sit there and be quiet."

The little girl cries.

"You know what you're acting like? A little brat!" She closes the door, says to herself, "Thank God I have the nanny tomorrow." Then she sees Bill watching, gives him an indignant look and climbs into the driver's seat, slams the door. She backs up without caution, the SUV's tires squealing as she pulls out of the lot.

Bill goes back to struggling with the carts, straining his weak muscles to get them stacked neatly in three, long rows.

White Shirt pokes his head out of the door. "Hurry up and get back inside. We need you on the floor."

The air conditioning is a relief. He hangs the oversized safety vest on a hook in the breakroom and makes his way back to the sales floor. Three supervisors crowd the manager's office, gossiping about staff and laughing.

"You'll cover two areas," says White Shirt. "We're shorthanded."

"Maybe if some of the supervisors helped out—"

"Don't question things, Bill. You've got to go with the flow if you want to be here for a while."

I'd rather die, he thinks, than waste my life here.

"Look sharp."

The questions keep coming. A young hipster wants to know which camera is best for YouTube. A middle-aged man comes in looking for business software. And a thirty-something account executive demands to speak with a manager when Bill can't tell him why the tablet he wants to buy was cheaper last week.

He's helping a young mother find a memory card for her camera when a man in a golf shirt interrupts. "Excuse me. Can you help me?"

"I'm sorry, sir. I'm helping this customer. I'll be glad to help you next."

"Your customer service around here sucks!"

"We're understaffed, sir. I'm trying my best." He feels the frustration boiling up beneath his skin, works to stay calm. He goes back to helping the mother.

"Get your manager, son. Now!"

He talks into his little radio. White Shirt comes bobbing down the aisle.

The next shift they call him into the office. The store manager waves him over to a big desk. "Have a seat in that chair, Bill."

"We're worried," says a supervisor, "about your customer service performance."

"Oh?"

"We've had a lot of complaints." The manager leans forward, rests both elbows on the desk. "We need to see immediate improvement if you want to continue as part of our team."

He wants to explode, to say what's on his mind and tell these dumb middle-management motherfuckers where they can put their shitty job, but he restrains himself and swallows hard. "I'm sorry."

White Shirt chimes in. "It just doesn't seem like you're committed to being here."

"I need this job. Please don't fire me."

The manager smiles. "That's all we wanted to hear, Bill."

34.

Ty's heart races. He takes the corner hard—almost goes down—jumps a planter box and keeps running. Tires screech, Oscar speeding to the back of the apartment complex. Maybe, Ty thinks, we can cut him off before he makes the fence. He digs in harder, his tattered Vans gripping the pavement.

Their target is Ben Wallace. Ben gave his girlfriend a solid beating—sixteen stitches and a night in the emergency room. Oscar bailed him out of county lockup on a $20,000 bond. Then he disappeared, didn't check in with the office, never showed in court. His mother put them in touch with an ex-girlfriend who was quick to roll on him for the hundred dollar bill Oscar waved in her face. But she had a change of heart, stalled them at the front door, and Ben escaped through a rear window. Now Ty's twenty feet behind him, closing the distance. What he'll do when he catches up, he's not exactly sure, but he readies himself for a fight.

A car swings up from the right—Oscar in the old Buick. Ben trips, goes down hard, and Ty's on top of him.

"You're under arrest!" he shouts. His breath is heavy; sweat pours down his forehead and neck. He pulls the handcuffs from his back pocket, snaps one around the left wrist.

Ben breaks free with the other hand, rolls onto his side and comes up swinging. But Oscar's there, dropping to the ground, pinning his arm down and helping Ty get him cuffed.

They sit him up. He spits, coughs.

"Is that how you treat the man who bailed you out of jail?"

"Fuck you and your blonde little bitch!"

"You mean the blonde little bitch who outran you?"

"I tripped. You guys got lucky." He spits again, a big wad of tobacco and saliva splattering inches from Oscar's shoe.

"Look," says Oscar, "that shit just ain't nice. You wanna keep spitting? I can call the deputies, arrange a ride to county in a paddy wagon—and you know the kind of treatment they dish out in the back of the paddy wagon."

Ben stares at him. Oscar continues, "Or you could play nice, take a ride in the plush backseat of my Buick. Hell, you pull that stick outta your ass and cooperate, I'd consider writing you another bond, get you back in your girl's bed in no time. You'd rather sleep with your girl, right? Or do you like fighting with four dudes over two bunks?"

Ben drops his head low between his shoulders, spreads his legs out on the pavement in defeat. "You got me," he says. "It's over."

Oscar slaps him on the shoulder. "That's what I like to hear, Ben. That's exactly what I like to hear."

An old, leathery-faced waitress comes around with a coffee pot. She smiles at Ty. "Here you go, kiddo."

He reads her nametag. "Thanks, Jeanne."

She winks and walks away.

"You sure get a lot of love from the waitresses, kid."

"Yeah, but she's not as cute as the last one."

"You call that girl yet?"

"Nah, but I've been texting her."

"Texting? There ain't no romance anymore." Oscar pours a shot from his flask into each of their cups. "Let's celebrate."

"Celebrate?"

"Here's to your first handcuffing, kid."

"I don't know," says Ty. "You helped. Does it still count?"

"Hell yeah, it counts. You had that guy, no problem." Oscar takes a big sip of his coffee. "I'm proud of you, kid. You're learning."

Ty takes a little sip. "Just think, if I didn't lose that bag of weed, I probably wouldn't even be here right now—would never have gone back to your office."

"True." Oscar shifts around in the bench seat. "But I think life has a way of working out—what's meant to happen will happen—if we let it. When I first came to the United States, for many years I was unhappy. But I made a life. A business. A house for my wife and daughters. Is it what I wanted?" He laughs. "Of course not. Does it make me happy? Yes, it makes me very happy."

"What are you saying, Oscar?"

Oscar thinks for a moment, takes another stiff sip. "I took your weed."

"Huh?"

"The night you came to my office."

"I left it there?"

"You never put it back in your pocket. Hell, you were so fucking stoned, it's no surprise you forgot."

"But when I came to your office the second time I asked you—" Ty gives him a pleading look, hoping that none of this is true.

"I lied to you."

Ty looks down at the table, plays with the silverware.

"You gonna say something?"

He doesn't look up.

"Ty?"

"Why are you telling me this now?"

"Because we're partners. We gotta be honest with each other, even when it's uncomfortable."

"Partners?"

"Yeah, kid. I'm gonna teach you everything I know. I've got your back and you've got mine."

"Is that really how you feel?"

Oscar nods.

"It's just a bag of weed, Oscar. Thanks for telling me the truth. I was going crazy wondering where I lost it."

Oscar leans over the table, gives him a firm slap on the shoulder. "I gotta hit the men's room. When that old waitress comes back, order us some more pie, will ya?"

He can only sit and smile.

35.

Elmo waits for the light to change then makes a left on Broadway. He parks the car on a side street—damn those Denver parking meters—and lights a cigarette. People pass in the night, hipsters and yuppie-tech-geeks and kids all trying to out-cool each other. A merry group pedal by on cruiser bikes. He catches fragments of their excited conversations, watches them move like one pulsing organism, red safety lights flashing down the street. The cigarette burns down and he lights another, walks up the block to the nightclub where a man called Small works the door.

There's a sign in the window: Enter in rear.

He walks around back to the alley, cowboy boots shuffling through gravel and dirt. A metal staircase clings to the exterior of the old brick building, winds up five stories to a rooftop party deck. Fuck, he thinks, I hate heights.

He makes his way slow and steady, looks down once or twice on the way up and almost gets sick. At the top, a pair of bouncers in black shirts check ID's. Elmo says something about being too old for ID then shows a fake Florida driver's license with a bullshit last name.

The bouncer checks the ID, looks up at Elmo, then back to the ID in his hand. "Your name really Elmore?"

"It's Elmo. People call me Elmo."

"Elmo," says the bouncer, "like Sesame Street?"

"Like Sesame Street. And what do they call a big guy like you?"

The bouncer smiles. "They call me Small."

"I imagine they do. Nice to meet you, Small."

"Pleasure's mine." Small gives a little salute and hands back the ID. "Be cool now."

Elmo laughs. "I'm always cool."

He sits at the bar next a pretty girl and orders a whiskey from a hurried bartender. When the drink finally comes he takes a stiff sip and goes to light a cigarette.

"You can't smoke here," says the girl.

"We're on the roof."

"It's still a club, and you can't smoke in a club. Where you from?"

"Texas, where we smoke wherever we damn well want."

She pulls the cherry from her drink, crushes it between perfect front teeth. "What brings you to Denver?"

"Business."

"What kind of business you in?"

"I solve problems for people."

"Problems?"

"Yes," he says, "problems of a certain nature."

"I get it, you like to be mysterious. But aren't you a little too old to be out tonight?" She doesn't wait for an answer. "Let me guess. You're some kind of salesman—industrial lubricant or some other horribly boring thing—and you're in town for a conference, one of those shitty, once a year events where all the salesmen jerk each other off and go out drinking afterward. Except they all went to the stripclub, and you wound up here, looking for a little local action."

Elmo chuckles, takes another sip of his drink. "Well that's a sad little story you've spun up, darlin', but it's far from the truth."

"Well in that case, what kind of problems do you solve?"

"Can I trust you?" He lowers his voice to a whisper.

She leans in. "I'll never see you again."

"Okay," he says. "I kill people. Or hurt them very badly."

She's quiet, doesn't move except to swish the ice around in the bottom of her glass. "Elmo, you really are a naughty conventioneer, telling me something dangerous and steamy like that. You trying to get between my legs?"

"You don't believe me?"

"Should a young woman ever believe an old man?"

"I guess not."

She puts her empty glass down on the bar. "Buy me another drink?"

"Forget it," says Elmo. "You're not even fun."

She gives him a hurt look and he ignores her, leaves a tip on the counter and gets up to walk away.

"You're just gonna leave me? What kind of gentleman are you?"

"I ain't no kind of gentleman." He walks to the other side of the dance floor, pushes past a sloppy drunk and takes a seat in a white, upholstered lounge chair. The girl at the bar slides up to the next guy, flirts for another drink.

It's two hours before Small takes a break. Elmo waits a minute, follows him back down the metal stairs, watches him go to the far end of the alley and open the door of an old Honda Civic hatchback.

Elmo lights another cigarette, walks up slowly to the car. There's the flash of a lighter and he smells weed. Fuckin' stoners.

Small sees him standing outside the car and rolls down the window. "Hey, Elmo. What's the good word?"

"You sharing?"

"Sure," says the big man. "Climb in."

Elmo goes around to the passenger side and opens the door. The seat is covered in trash.

"Sorry it's so messy, man. I meant to clean it." Small brushes empty wrappers and soda cans onto the floor and offers Elmo a green and yellow pipe. "You lookin' to get hooked up? Try this shit—fucking awesome. Go ahead, man, hit that shit."

He closes the door, waves off the pipe. "That's not really what I wanted."

"What the fuck, man?"

Elmo pulls his knife from a pocket, clicks it open and let's Small get a good look at the blade.

"I thought you were cool."

"Listen to me." Elmo snaps his fingers. "Hey, this is important. I need your little marijuana-mush-brain to focus."

"You robbin' me?"

"Vicky Lipinski," says Elmo.

Small looks confused. "You know Vicky?"

"You're going to drive me to her."

"Sorry, I can't do that."

"Look, it's been a long day, and I've got a headache from that shitty dance music you kids play. I'll spare you a long-winded speech about how scary I am, about how I'll cut your dick off and sew it inside your mouth if you don't do what I say. I'll get right to the point, Small. I've killed motherfuckers much bigger than you with a knife much smaller than this. Now I'll ask you again: Where the fuck is Vicky Lipinski?"

"I don't know," says Small. His hands shake. "I haven't seen her for about a month."

"Bullshit!" Elmo reaches out with the knife, slashes it through the air for effect. "Her parents said you're the boyfriend."

"Parents? I ain't never met Vicky's parents, and I sure as fuck ain't Vicky's boyfriend. We smashed on occasion, don't get me wrong, but Vicky ain't really the relationship type. You know what I'm saying?"

"You're saying she's a slut." He remembers the Instagram pictures of Vicky in her tiny bikini, a beer in hand.

"I prefer the term free-spirited."

"I don't care what you prefer. You're gonna take me to her place or this knife goes between your ribs."

"Fuck you, man. I don't appreciate your aggressive energy coming in my car and interrupting my peaceful flow and shit."

"Fuck your flow, Small. This is about Vicky. Now, if you want money—"

"Money?"

"Sure, isn't that what a guy like you is all about? Those Air Jordans ain't gonna buy themselves."

"How much?"

"Finally, a man with sense." Elmo flashes a wide grin. "You take me to Vicky Lipinski, the boss gives you an even thousand."

"Dollars?"

"No, Mexican Pesos." Elmo decides that he hates Small.

"Just checking."

"But you gotta drive me right to Vicky and wait while I call the boss. Then you get paid, cash money."

Small starts the car and Elmo goes to send a text to Tony. He's looking down at the screen, struggling with the buttons, when Small jams his foot into the accelerator and the car jumps to life. Then the bouncer braces hard and smashes the brake pedal, throws Elmo forward and off balance. Small's hand goes beneath the seat, comes up with a shiny handgun.

Elmo doesn't stop to think. He throws his weight into Small's body, jams the knife into soft flesh. Small cries out in pain and grabs at his side. Blood runs between his fingers and he looks up at Elmo, a shocked expression on his face. But Elmo doesn't wait. He opens the passenger door and runs from the car, Small screaming into the empty night. "I'll kill you, motherfucker! I'll kill you!"

Elmo hears the first shot and drops to the ground. There's another shot. Then another. Something stings his arm. Heat spreads from his shoulder across his chest and down his back. With the strength of one arm, he pulls himself into a gap between two buildings and collapses into a struggling heap of sweat and blood and breath. Moments later he hears the sirens.

No time to rest. He climbs to his feet, balances himself with a hand on the dark red brickwork. Then he's rounding the corner, rolling his sleeve up around the wound to absorb and conceal the blood. Four blocks, he thinks. They'll set the perimeter at four blocks.

He walks eight long blocks, counting each one aloud, and ducks into a narrow alley where he crouches behind a dumpster and struggles again with the phone. It rings. Answer, damn it. Answer.

"Hello?"

"Eddie?"

"Elmo, what's going on?"

"I'm shot," he says. "Cops all over the place. You gotta pick me up."

36.

Eddie drives. Elmo rides shotgun in the passenger seat. He holds a towel over his shot-up arm with his free hand, works to maintain pressure.

Eddie's phone rings. "Tony? It's me—Eddie."

"Don't talk and drive," says Elmo. "It's dangerous." He laughs when he thinks about how ridiculous that sounds, coming from a guy with a throbbing bullet wound.

"It's bad, Tony. He's bleeding all over the fucking car. What? Sheldon's place?" Eddie takes his hand off the wheel and the car jerks to one side before he recovers. "Alright," he says. "Yeah—ten minutes."

"Don't wreck the fucking car, Eddie. Focus."

"How about you drive then, huh?"

"I will if you don't shut the fuck up and quit looking over at me. Watch the road."

"Okay, okay," says Eddie. "Relax. You're gonna be fine."

"Where are we going, anyway?"

"A mortuary."

Stanley Family Mortuary occupies an historic stone mansion at the corner of York and 16th. They turn off Colfax into the back alley and a garage door rumbles open. A thin man with high, stiff cheek-bones waves them inside. He wears a shiny black smock and a pair of purple rubber gloves. "Oh, dear," he says, "what happened?"

"A little mishap," says Eddie. "You ready for us?"

"Oh, yes. I cleared the table right after Tony called."

"Good. Help me get him inside."

They help Elmo stagger—one of them under each arm—past of row of gurneys to a narrow door in the back of the garage. He looks up in time to notice an embalmed corpse spread out on one of the gurneys, an old woman, someone's grandma, in a cheap dress and a paper tag on one toe.

The embalming room is cramped. A row of base cabinets line the wall, the counter covered in towels and metal instruments. Elmo sees a rusty scalpel and a handsaw with tiny bits of white bone still stuck to the ragged blade. In the center of the room is a porcelain table, a styrofoam block at one end. They slide him onto the table, position the block beneath his neck and head. Then the man in the shiny black apron is leaning over him, looking down, a bright fluorescent light behind him.

"Go ahead and pass out," says the man. "What I'm about to do will hurt."

He dreams of machine gun fire and boys running through a thick jungle in another time and place. One of them looks at him and says, "I want to go home, Elmo. I don't want to die." Tears swell in the boy's eyes. Then a bullet rips through his dirty neck and his body spins to the ground.

"Elmo! Elmo!" Someone else is calling him.

"I'm here," he says. "I'm here."

But when he opens his eyes it's only Tony, standing over him, shouting his name.

Elmo sits on a gurney in the funeral home's garage. A single yellow bulb, suspended by a thin chain, lights the room. There's a corpse on another gurney behind him, a neat little bullet wound in the right temple.

"Suicide," says the man in the black apron. "Nothing to worry about. You're safe here." He pulls off a rubber glove and extends a hand. "Sheldon Stanley, third generation funeral director and embalmer."

"Oh, shit. Your parents named you Sheldon Stanley?"

"The Third," he says, "Sheldon Stanley the Third."

"I'm guessing it was you who saved my life?"

Tony bounces back into the room through a side door. "Sure was!" He hands Elmo a lighter and a fresh pack of cigarettes. "You gave me a real fucking scare, pal. What happened out there?"

"I brought a knife to a gunfight."

"Big mistake. I'm always telling you to get a pistol. Maybe now you'll listen."

"You know I don't like guns."

"It's the noise," Tony tells Sheldon, "ever since Vietnam."

Elmo ignores him and lights a cigarette. He inspects the bandage on his arm, the spot of dried blood. "How bad it is? You think I'll lose the arm?"

"Nothing to worry about." Sheldon smiles dimly and wipes his hands on his apron. "I irrigated the wound, sutured the skin, and applied sterile dressing. It's nothing a little rest won't help."

Elmo whistles. "Damn, Doc. Where'd you learn to do all that?"

The stiff little man smiles wider. "Living flesh or dead, it's all the same to me."

Tony pulls a small flask from his back pocket and takes a sip. "Who did this, pal? Huh? Who fucking did this to you? Tell me and they're fucking dead."

"Some kid, a bouncer at the club—the one from Vicky Lipinski's Instagram."

"The boyfriend?"

"Not according to him. He says he ain't seen Vicky in a month. Says she's a wild one, too hot to handle."

"It still don't add up," says Tony. He takes another sip and lights a cigarette. "First the girl drops out of sight and then Ulibarri goes missing—now some punk kid puts a bullet in your arm?"

"What are you saying, Tony?"

"Maybe," Tony paces, shiny leather shoes grinding on concrete, "that cheater Ulibarri wasn't really kidnapped at all. Maybe he fucked that girl, Vicky Lipinski, at a party or in some nasty alley, and recruited her to set the whole thing up—to hide from me—to get away with my money."

"And he needed me," says Elmo, "to witness the kidnapping. How else would word get back to you?"

"He knew I'd send someone out to collect. Guys like me always send someone."

"Yes," says Elmo, "but how did he know when I'd be coming?"

Tony takes a few shallow drags from his cigarette. "Someone had to tell him." He stops pacing, drops the cigarette to the ground and stamps it out with the toe of his shoe. "Where's Eddie?" He looks around the room, his face turning red. He pounds on an empty gurney and screams. "Find me fucking Eddie!"

37.

Bill wants to go home. The store is closing and it's been a long shift. There's a squawk in his ear, the supervisor calling him back to the office.

"Bill, we're going to need you to stay late tonight."

"But I've been here since opening."

"I know, Bill, and I really hate to do this to you. One of the stockers called in sick and we've got that big sale tomorrow."

"I'm not a stocker. That's not my job."

"We're a team here, Bill."

"Really?"

"I don't want to have to force you," says the supervisor, "but it's right there, in the written policy."

"Unbelievable."

"Is there a problem? It wouldn't hurt to show a little dedication."

You don't pay me enough, Bill thinks, to show dedication. "How late do you need me?"

"One. Two. Whenever the work gets done."

"Two o'clock in the morning! You're serious?"

"I'm serious." The supervisor rocks back in his chair. "But you can come in late tomorrow. We're not about to pay you overtime."

38.

Dylan sucks on a tall strawberry milkshake. "I can't believe you brought me to a diner."

Ty digs for the cherry with his straw. "Why not?"

"Because I work at a diner, silly."

"I know. I just thought you might like getting served for a change."

"They have servers at nice restaurants." She kicks him hard in the shin beneath the table.

"I'm sorry," he says. "We can go somewhere else if you want."

"I don't know." She looks down at her milkshake. "This is pretty fucking good."

The old waitress comes by; Dylan gets an omelet and Ty orders a Monte Cristo. "Extra powdered sugar, please."

"Sure thing, sweetie."

Dylan gets out of the booth and sits down on his side, nudges him over and slides up close. "So you're really a bounty hunter?"

"Bail enforcement." He nods. "That's the technical term. But I'll be writing bonds soon."

"And that old guy, the one you were eating with, he's your boss?"

"You mean Oscar? We're partners."

She gives him a little punch on the elbow. "Ever been in a fight?"

"Yep. Just the other day we tackled a guy and I took a punch to the face."

"Sexy," she says. "Maybe we can hit the ring some time."

"You box?"

"Picked it up in San Francisco. There's a gym I go to on East Colfax."

He laughs again. "Shit, you'd kick my ass. I only know a few dirty tricks that Oscar showed me."

"Do they work?"

"So far."

The waitress comes back with their food and Ty gets powdered sugar all over his shirt and Dylan laughs and almost spits up milkshake.

"You wanna go back to your place, maybe chill for a while?"

He remembers the dirty dishes stacked up in the kitchen, the pile of clothes on the living room floor. "Uh—"

"Come on. I wanna see where you live. I don't care if it's messy." She pulls at his tank top.

"How'd you know?"

"I have brothers. Boys are messy."

"It's not far," he says. "I'll get the check."

He closes the door behind them and goes to the kitchen counter, starts tidying up. He moves quickly to the living room, grabs a dirty pair of underwear from the couch and flings them into a corner. "I'm sorry, my roommate is such a pig."

"I like it." She shrugs. "Is your roommate here?"

"Bill? No, he works pretty late. And it takes him an hour to ride the bus home."

"Oh, then we're all alone. Got any wine?"

He laughs. "I think Bill keeps a box in the refrigerator. He likes to drink a glass when he reads something fancy. But I say there's nothing fancy about wine in a box."

"You're probably right, but I'll still drink it."

He rummages through the kitchen cabinets for a clean glass, finds a couple of plastic cups and fills them each from a little nozzle.

"My lady." He hands her a cup.

"Thank you, sir. Who knew you could be such a gentleman?"

"Not even my own mother."

She makes a mischievous face. "Got any weed?"

"Damn, girl. You're getting right to the point."

"You smoke, right?"

"Well, yeah—"

"Then what's the problem?"

"It's just, normally, girls aren't too excited about weed."

"Then you're hanging out with the wrong girls."

He goes to Bill's room and comes back with a cardboard shoebox. He grinds a nug and packs the sticky weed into a yellow and blue pipe, the one Bill gave him last year for his birthday. "You first."

She takes the first hit and sinks back into the cushions. Then he takes a hit and sinks back next to her.

"Hey," she says, "truth or dare?"

"I pick truth."

"What's the wildest sexual experience you've ever had?"

"Damn."

"You afraid to tell me? Maybe you're a virgin?"

"Okay, I'll play." He looks around like someone else might be in the room. "I hooked up with a guy at a party once. We made out and I woke up in bed with him."

She looks surprised. "Did you fuck him?"

"I can't remember. I was drunk and high on coke."

"A true bohemian." She nods at a stack of books along the wall, a sketchbook perched on top. "Next you'll tell me you're an artist." She walks over and picks it up, thumbs through the pages. Planets and monsters and fantastic creatures are drawn in pencil with finely shaded details.

"It's nothing," he says. "I just mess around."

"Ty, these are really good."

He grabs a cushion and pulls it in front of him, blocks his face from view. "This is so embarrassing."

"Stop it. You have real talent. Have you shown these to anyone?"

"Just a professor in college. He told me they were juvenile and a waste of artistic talent."

"I see." She stares at a page then looks up to where he's still hiding behind the cushion. "Don't let one dumb professor kill your confidence. I'm telling you, these are awesome. We're gonna put together a portfolio and post it online."

"We are?"

"Yeah, I'll help you. I'm studying to be an art director. I know good work when I see it."

"You really mean it? You'd help me like that?"

"Yeah, but only because you're cute." She walks back to the couch, climbs on top of him. "Now make out with me."

They make out and talk about art and she tells him about her little brothers and how hard her mom works to support them. He warms some taquitos in the oven and they curl up to watch a movie. It's late when they fall asleep, wrapped in each other's arms.

The door bursts open at three in the morning and the light comes on in the kitchen. Bill stands in the middle of the room in a sweaty blue polo shirt. "Do you have any idea what I've been through tonight?"

"Bill?"

"Wake the fuck up, you won't believe what happened." Bill goes over to the lamp, the living room fills with light. "Oh, who's the girl?"

"My friend Dylan."

"I don't give a fuck who she is. Just listen to this."

"Hey, that's not polite."

Dylan rubs her eyes. "It's okay."

"I'm sorry," says Ty. "He's not normally this level of rude."

"Yes, I'm sorry." Bill paces on the stained carpet. "Anyway, I was saying—those motherfuckers at the store kept me five hours late to stock shelves for the big sale tomorrow."

"Why didn't you tell them no?"

"They basically told me that if I didn't stay, I'd be fired. I'm telling you, Ty, I can't take this corporate bullshit."

"So quit."

"Are you crazy? Here's the worst part: I'm standing on Colorado Boulevard, waiting for the bus, when I realize it's Sunday. The bus doesn't run that late on Sunday. So I had to walk, six fucking miles, after seventeen long hours on my feet."

"I'm sorry, Bill. Really, why don't you quit? You can find something else."

"Like what? What else am I gonna do?"

"Write an article, or a story. Dylan's gonna help me with a portfolio. You could do the same thing."

"Um—"

"Write about your job—about the uninspiring conditions of the underemployed youth of America."

Dylan chimes in. "I'm with Ty."

Bill says, "I don't even know you."

She smiles at him. "Are you even a real writer?"

He looks at Ty, a dead expression on his face. "Who is this girl?"

"She's awesome, right?"

"Yeah," says Bill. "Awesome." He squeezes between the two of them on the couch. "What are we watching?"

39.

Eddie's in an empty garage, positioned in the center of the room over a floor drain. His arms and legs are bound to a metal chair with duct tape; his mouth is gagged. Air wheezes in and out of his thick nose.

"Hey, dumbass!" Tony's deep laughter erupts from the open doorway. "You really are an idiot. I gave you a good job—brought you into the family—and you fucked me. What am I gonna tell my sister?"

Elmo peels back a corner of the tape on Eddie's face. "Here's the deal, I'm gonna pull this tape off your mouth, and when I do, it's really gonna fuckin' hurt. But it ain't nothing like the hurt you're gonna feel if you don't answer my questions. Understood?"

Eddie gives a nervous nod.

"One. Two." Elmo rips the tape hard.

Eddie shouts, lurches forward in agony. "Fuck! What's this all about?"

"What's it all about?" Tony puts a hand on his shoulder. "How about the way you double-crossed me to that motherfucker Ulibarri? How much was your cut?"

Eddie looks back and forth between the two Texans. "I got no idea what you're talking about. You're family, Tony. I would never do that to you."

Elmo lights a cigarette, takes a drag and holds the glowing cancer stick an inch from Eddie's eyeball. "There's a problem, Eddie. Don Ulibarri knew we were coming, and you were the only one besides me and the boss-man who could have told him. But there's more, Eddie, because then I go to see Vicky Lipinski's dumbass friend and he shoots me in the fucking arm. I could have died, Eddie. Doesn't all of that seem a little odd? Or is Denver just that fucking weird?"

Eddie squirms and cries. "I swear I don't got nothin' to do with it. You gotta believe me. I swear on my sweet mother's grave. Bless her soul."

"Look, I wanna believe you. But Tony here wants to be sure you ain't lying. And he's a harder guy to convince."

"How do I prove it to you? Tell me. Anything."

"Oh," says Elmo, "you don't have to do a thing. I'll do all the work." He takes another long drag of his cigarette, blows the smoke in Eddie's face and pulls a pair of slender pliers from his back pocket.

"What are those for?" Eddie squirms in the chair.

"Getting to the truth." He clamps the tip of the pliers down on Eddie's fingernail and snaps back in one clean motion, waves the bloody mess around in front of Eddie's face.

Eddie screams as blood fills the wound on his finger.

"Fucking maniac." He pants heavily, struggles to breathe. "I thought we were friends." Tears cover his round face.

"See, that was your mistake. I don't have any friends." Elmo comes down with the pliers again, this time it's the ring finger. Eddie screams and wriggles but the tape holds tight. "Tell us what you fucking did, Eddie." Another snap of his arm and the nail jerks free of the finger.

Another scream.

Eddie's shirt is soaked with sweat. The veins in his forehead throb, his skin a dark shade of red. "Please," he sobs, "I'm begging you. I don't know anything! I swear I don't know anything!"

Elmo brings the pliers down again. Eddie screams and wails and rocks the chair back and forth.

"Did you tell that fucker Small I was coming? Did you tell him to fucking shoot me?" Elmo gets a good grip on a fingernail. "Ten fingers, then it's onto the toes." He smiles. "You can't imagine—"

Tony steps in between them. "We're wasting our time with this bullshit. Let's kill him and go for a beer." He reaches down to his boot, comes back up with a shiny silver pistol and puts the barrel of the gun to Eddie's temple. "Tell the motherfucking truth."

Eddie's hysterical. He's sobbing and weeping and snot hangs from his swollen nostrils. A dark spot spreads across his crotch. He mutters something about loving his wife.

"Fuck, Eddie. You made me do this."

Eddie closes his eyes tight, thinks about his girls and hopes they'll be okay without him.

Tony pulls the trigger.

Click! The hammer falls but the gun doesn't fire. Elmo watches in silence.

Eddie doesn't breathe, doesn't dare to open his eyes.

"Okay, you didn't do it." Tony drops the pistol to his side.

Eddie opens his eyes, looks around. "You're not going to kill me?"

"I know you, Eddie. If you knew anything you would have cracked."

Elmo gets to work unwrapping the duct tape.

"Oh, God!" Eddie's hands and feet and arms and legs and whole body are shaking from head to toe. "You almost fucking killed me." He clutches his bloody fingers.

"Don't be a baby, Eddie. It's just business. Elmo's gonna take you to see Sheldon, get your hand all wrapped up." Tony gives him a big slap on the shoulder. "We've got work to do and I'm gonna need you."

Eddie leans forward, rests his elbows on his knees and works to calm himself. He stares up at both of them, Elmo looking serious and Tony smiling. "Can I get a drink or something? You scared the shit out of me."

"Sure," says Tony, "I owe you one. But first you need a new pair of pants."

40.

They're in the old Buick again. This time Ty drives and Oscar rides shotgun, puffing on a cigarillo. "I'm telling you, kid, ain't no reason to get all crazy about this girl when you just met her. Take it slow."

Ty turns the car onto Bannock, heads south from the Downtown Detention Center. "I'm not crazy. She's just—cool, you know?"

"They're all cool at first."

"Dylan is different. She's beautiful and acts like one of the guys—doesn't even care about my smelly feet."

"Damn, maybe she is different. It's like my wife, she pops the zits on my back." He blows smoke through the cracked window. "That's true love."

At the next light he tells Ty to turn right, then a quick left into the first parking lot, a little jewelry store with sale prices on the windows in yellow paint. "Wait in the car."

"What's this? You robbing the place?"

"No, dumbass. I'm getting an anniversary ring for my wife."

"Oh, Oscar! That's so sweet. Can I come? I wanna see."

"No, you can't come. Wait here."

"Why not?"

"Because if the salesman starts showing me something fancier, something more expensive, you'll say it looks better and guilt me into buying it."

"Oscar!"

"Just wait here, kid. There's a joint wrapped up in a plastic bag in the glove compartment. Help yourself."

Ty watches Oscar go into the store then digs around for the joint. He lights it and cracks the window, puts his shoes up on the passenger seat. The sun beats down through the open window and warms his face.

Oscar comes back in a few minutes. "Get those filthy shoes off my seat."

Ty grins. "I wanna see."

"Alright, but if you say anything to the wife about this you're a dead man." He opens a velvet-wrapped jewelry box. Inside is a silver ring, inset with a row of sparkling diamonds.

"It's beautiful."

Oscar snaps the lid shut and hides the little jewelry box in the back of the glove compartment behind some papers and an old stick of deodorant. "Come on, kid. We gotta get back to work. You better not be too high."

"I do my best work high."

"Yeah, alright. Just save some of that for me."

"Where are we going anyway?"

"All the way out to Castle Rock—got an easy pickup." He relights the joint and takes a deep hit. "Think, what's the first place a scared bail jumper goes when he's got nowhere else to turn?"

"Mom's house."

"Exactly. They always go to mommy." Oscar laughs. "In this case, mommy is a stand-up citizen. She called me right away to report her son."

"How much did you have to bribe her?"

"Nothing. She's a real do-gooder. Rolled on her son free of charge."

"Damn. I hope my mom wouldn't do that to me. Laws come and go but family is forever."

"I didn't realize you were so family-oriented."

"Huh?"

"Let's just get back to the case." He sucks the last of the joint, tosses the roach out the window. "It's simple. We park outside the house and call mom. She brings our guy out and we hook him up. So long, mommy."

"And then we get milkshakes?"

"Yeah, kid. Then we get milkshakes. But this time I'm not gonna let you take any phone numbers. This girl, Dylan, she's distracting you."

"You think I'm distracted?" He rolls his eyes. "Is that why you let me drive?"

"No, I let you drive so I could do this." He unscrews the cap on his metal flask, takes a long sip.

"Shit," says Ty, "you're hopeless."

It's an hour's ride, passing first through Denver's outer suburbs, then up and over a series of rolling hills and down into the commuter's paradise of Castle Rock—land of outlet malls and over-mortgaged faux-luxury homes. They take the last exit and head for an older part of town. Oscar checks the map on his phone, guides Ty to a gravelly street lined with ranch homes. They park beneath the dark shadow of a tree in a cul-de-sac at the end of the road.

Oscar dials a number on his phone. "Yes, Mrs. Turner. It's Oscar Martinez from Martinez Bail Bonds. I'm parked outside with my partner."

Ty tries to hear what she's saying on the other end of the call.

Oscar continues, "Yes, Mrs. Turner. Tell him you called a lawyer, you're taking him over there now. Yes, ma'am, we're ready."

They wait twelve long minutes, then the front door opens, the mom walking out with the son behind her. She goes around to the driver's side of a white Nissan Altima and opens the door.

Oscar bangs on the dash. "Now, kid! Block 'em in."

Ty starts the engine, drops it into drive and burns rubber. The Buick screeches to a stop diagonally behind the Altima and Oscar jumps out of the passenger side.

"You're under arrest!" he shouts. "Get down on the ground and keep your hands out!"

Ty bounces from his seat and runs to join Oscar. They each grab an arm and wrestle their fugitive down to the ground—get the handcuffs on. After a quick search they sit him up against a dirty tire, hands behind his back.

"Alex Turner—" Oscar stands over their catch. "You're officially busted." He holds out a legal document with signatures and stamps along the bottom.

Alex twists around, looks up at his mom. "How could you do this to me? How could you send me back to jail?"

"I'm sorry," she says, "but you have to deal with this, Alex. It's too big to go away." She drops her gaze to the ground then back to her son, makes eye contact. "It's better now than later. You're in enough trouble already."

Oscars pulls him up by the arm. "It's time to go."

Alex pleads. "Please don't take me back to jail." Tears roll down his cheeks. "You can't take me back there. I can't make it one night in that place."

"You didn't go to court, Alex."

"I'm sorry." Alex is shaking. "I got scared. Can I please have a cigarette?"

Oscar nods his head. "Hey kid, grab the guy a smoke, will ya?"

Ty brings him a cigarette, puts it between his lips and lights it. Then they walk him over to the car, buckle him into the back seat. "It's a long drive," says Ty. "Don't give us any trouble."

Up and over the hills, back through manicured suburbs with their walking trails and community centers and neighborhood watch associations. Oscar gives Alex another cigarette, humming an old Mexican song while he lights one for himself. "I'm hungry," he says. "Let's pull off and get something to eat. There's a Steak 'n Shake out here somewhere."

Ty gets off the highway at County Line, heads west. "They've got milkshakes, right?"

"Yeah, kid, whatever you want. But get a steakburger. I'm getting two or three." He takes a drag and turns to Alex. "Listen, you promise not to do anything stupid and I'll move those cuffs around to the front, buy you a decent lunch. You ain't getting no steakburgers in jail."

Alex nods. "I promise. Sitting on these handcuffs really hurts."

They turn into the parking lot; the drive-through line is wrapped around the building and onto a side street.

"Just park the car, kid. I'll go inside for the food and we can eat out here." Oscar leans Alex forward, undoes one of the handcuffs and brings them around front, snaps them back into place over Alex's wrist. "You be good." Then he walks across the parking lot, stamps out his cigarette before disappearing behind a smoked glass door.

Alex slumps in the backseat. Ty watches him in the rearview mirror. "Cheer up, man. It's not all bad. Things have a way of working out."

"Easy for you to say—you're not the one in handcuffs."

"What did you do?"

"Possession of heroin."

"First offense?"

"Second. The judge said if I he saw me in his courtroom again, I'd go to jail for a year."

"Then why didn't you show up for court?"

"I can't go to jail, man. I've got a little girl to feed, two years old." He hangs his head low, looks down at the floor.

"Can't you quit the heroin?"

"I tried," he says, "but it's amazing—heroin—takes all the pain away. I was clean coming out of jail the last time and went right back to it."

Ty is quiet for a minute, then he says, "I had a friend in high school who died from an overdose."

"Damn, man. That's some rough shit. I came close to overdosing once or twice, back when I was shooting, but now I mostly smoke the stuff."

"But you've got a daughter to feed—said it yourself."

"I haven't seen her in two months, you know? She's with her mom at her grandma's house. Grandma won't let me go near her." Alex fidgets with the handcuffs. "What am I gonna do now? Ain't no job for a two-time drug felon."

"There's gotta be something you can do."

"Hey, you mind if I have another cigarette?"

"Sure."

Oscar comes back to the car, hands Ty the drinks and food through the open window and climbs back into the backseat. "Pass me that soda." He wipes the sweat from his forehead with a napkin. "I got you a chocolate shake with an extra cherry."

They sit in the car and eat, no one saying much of anything. There's the sound of the air conditioner and the clinking of Alex's handcuffs, the muffled rattling of ice in styrofoam cups. Then Oscar tells Ty to drive. "You've got enough time," he says to Alex, "for a couple more cigarettes."

The Downtown Detention Center was designed by some unimaginative architect to look like a mid-rise office tower, with ugly, mud-colored walls and mirrored slits of glass that conceal from view the activity inside. Oscar presses a button on the intercom and they hand Alex over to another pair of deputies.

"Good luck," says Oscar.

Then the thick metal door swings shut and he's gone.

"Do you think he'll be okay?"

"I don't know, kid. Was he ever?"

"Isn't it kinda weird, taking people to jail for the same stuff we do?"

"How do you mean?"

"Weed," says Ty. "Alcohol. Tobacco. Money. It's all the same."

"It's not the same, because heroin is still illegal. Ain't nobody over-dosed on marijuana."

"Is any of this worth it?" Ty waves his hand at the jail, the muddy wall looming up behind him. "Police, courts, crowded jails, and pris-ons run for profit—is any of it really helping? Or are we all just keeping busy?"

"Look, kid, it's not our problem. Guys like us, we learn to play the system, work the angles and make our money. In the end it's all just business."

"It's not just business. These are real people, real lives."

"You had a tough case. It happens." Oscar lights another cigarette. "Sometimes it hits close to home. Now listen good to what I'm about to tell you. The people locked up inside those walls made their own choices. And that's what life's all about—the choices we make."

Ty shakes his head. "I don't know, Oscar."

"What the fuck is there to know? You wanna change the world? Go ahead. I'm putting food on my kid's plate every time, no matter what I gotta do, because my girls are my number one priority. You think a sad story from another hopeless addict is gonna get in the way of that? Grow up, kid. This is America. This is how it works."

"It just doesn't seem right."

"Nothing is right. Take a look around." Oscar straightens up, looks Ty in the eyes. "I love you, kid. Really, I fucking do. I took you under my wing and I'm teaching you everything I know. Are you in or are you out?"

Ty looks down at the sidewalk, shuffles his feet. "I don't know," he says. "I guess I'm out."

"All of this over a dumb fucking junkie—some kid throwing his life away for heroin?"

"It's more than that, Oscar. It's just—I'd rather be a part of the solution than the problem."

Oscar's face softens. "You're breakin' my fucking heart, kid. My stomach's all in knots." He takes a long drag. "You're like a son to me."

Ty snatches the cigarette from Oscar's lips. "You smoke too much."

Oscar chuckles, a quiet little broken laugh. He goes to light another and stops. "You want a ride?"

"It's not far," says Ty. "I'll walk."

It's late afternoon when Ty opens the door, walks with a heavy heart into the living room and drops himself onto the couch.

Bill comes in from the bedroom, pulls his blue uniform shirt over his head. "Hey, how was your pickup? You bust the guy?"

"Yeah, we busted him. But it didn't feel very good."

"What do you mean?"

"He was just like us, Bill. Just a kid. Could have been one of our friends."

"Sounds like a bad day." Bill walks over to the coffee table and picks up a pipe. "Come on, let's smoke it off. You'll feel better next time."

"There won't be a next time. I quit."

"But the money? You were making so much money—"

"Money made at the expense of others."

"What about rent?"

"We'll figure it out. We always do."

"Damn it." Bill looks at his watch and puts down the pipe. "I don't have time for this bullshit. I gotta get to work. You, with the admirable yet inconvenient sense of morality, find a fucking job. Take my laptop, get on Craigslist."

Ty grabs the pipe. "Sure, after I smoke."

"I'm serious, Ty. I can't be the only one around here with a sense of responsibility." He grabs his keys from the counter, marches across the living room to the front door.

"Have fun," says Ty. "I love you."

Bill slams the door behind him.

41.

"Fuck this fucking job!" Bill takes a long hit from a skinny joint, passes it back to Ryan. "Can you believe that asshole, telling me to clean the bathroom? Me? I'm a fucking writer. I've got a college degree, man."

"Yeah, but can you make rent?"

"Fuck! Pass me the pipe again."

Bill is laughing off his anger, mocking one of their supervisors, when they hear a woman scream. Then another man yells, "Call 911! Someone call 911!" They sneak around the corner of the building, see a man face down on the ground in the parking lot. A woman kneels beside him, crying and wailing his name. "Oh, my Truman! You're okay, Truman! Wake up!"

The man shouting for 911 spots Bill and Ryan along the curb. "You guys work here, do something!"

Bill sprints forward and drops to the pavement beside the unresponsive man. He remembers the summer lifeguard job he had in college. It was meant to be a way of meeting chicks, making a little easy cash, but now all that's running through his head is the training. "Help me roll him over. Let's get him on his back." He puts his ear next to the man's mouth and listens, hears nothing. "Okay, I'm going to give two breaths." He cups his mouth over the man's lips, pinches the nose with thumb and forefinger and tilts the head into position.

Then it's two big breaths. One. Two. He watches the man's chest rise and fall.

He shuffles down to the man's side, places both hands on top of the sternum and counts out loud. "One one-thousand. Two one-thousand." He thrusts down hard, compresses the rib cage and the heart. "Three one-thousand. Four one-thousand."

When he gets to thirty he stops counting, moves back up to the head and gives two more breaths. One. Two.

Then it's back to the chest and another round of thirty compressions. His arms get tired but he keeps going, ignores the burning in his muscles.

Someone brings him an AED from inside the store. He attaches the big sticky chest pads and the machine takes a reading. "SHOCK ADVISED!"

He presses a button.

The man's body jerks hard, his head slams from side to side. Vomit pours up from his mouth. Bill rolls the man onto his side, supports his head so the fluid can clear the airway.

The man coughs, gasps for air. His face turns bright red, little blood vessels bursting from the sudden return of pressure.

"He's breathing," says Bill. "He's breathing!"

That's when he hears the siren, sees the flashing lights pull into the parking lot. Two paramedics in white shirts take control of the scene. "Let's back it up," says the bigger one, "make some room."

Bill steps back and notices the crowd for the first time. People mill about, twisting their shoes into the pavement, talking amongst themselves and pointing. The store manager watches in his white shirt, his mouth hanging open.

Then it's over. The ambulance drives away and the crowd breaks up. A few minutes later Bill stands alone.

The manager comes over. "How'd you learn to do that?

"I was a lifeguard."

"He's lucky you were there. Time to get back to work."

"Could I just have a cigarette or something? My nerves are a little jumpy."

"Your break ended five minutes ago, and there's a new display to set up in the DVD aisle." He smiles at Bill, shakes a pointed finger. "Besides, smoking will kill you."

Bill gets to work assembling the cardboard display of a talking guinea pig. Ryan pops his head around the corner. "Hey, man. That was amazing! They should give you an award or something."

"They sent me back to work, told me to put together this movie display."

"That's bullshit, man. You're a fucking hero. Hey, if they were smart, they'd get it on the news, maybe bring some more people into the store."

"I had to help," says Bill. "I don't want to be on the news."

"Let's go smoke again. Come on, fuck 'em."

A supervisor walks by an aisle over, clears his throat.

"Go away," says Bill. He puts his head down, looks at the floor. "I gotta work."

The next morning they call him into the office. They wait for him to sit then the HR manager closes the door, takes her seat at the little round conference table and organizes her notes to avoid eye contact.

"Bill," she says, "after the incident yesterday in the parking lot, several people reported that you smelled like marijuana."

He doesn't say anything.

"We're going to need you to complete a drug test."

Bill thinks for a minute. "Why? Marijuana is legal in Colorado."

"Yes," she says, "but it's illegal according to the federal government, and still remains prohibited by our corporate policy. In the event of reasonable suspicion, the employee is required to submit to a drug test."

"This is insane. I saved a man's life out there and you want me to take a drug test? You don't know the first thing about how to treat your employees."

"You have until the end of the day," she says, "to report to our testing center."

"Forget it." He pushes his chair back and stands. "I'm worth more than this. I'm not subjugating myself to your fascist corporate regime."

Her face is blank. "So you're refusing?"

"Yes. I refuse."

"I'm sorry, Bill, but your employment with this company has been terminated. I'll need your badge and name tag."

The sliding doors swoosh closed behind him for the last time. It's a clear morning, the sun is shining. He listens to the sound of his own footsteps, feels the expansion and contraction of his breath. Cars pass by on the road. A mother waits with her children at the bus stop.

But he doesn't wait for the bus. His feet carry him home.

42.

Ty's on the couch, rolling a blunt on the coffee table. Bill opens the door, comes bursting into the apartment. "Where were you last night?"

"With Dylan at her place in Uptown." Ty frowns. "You gotta stop coming in like that. Relax, smoke this shit." He lights the blunt, takes a few puffs and passes it to Bill. "Dude, one of Dylan's roommates is perfect for you. She's an English major at Metro State and wants to move to New York, said Kerouac was her favorite writer."

"Predictable. They all say Kerouac." Bill drops to the couch next to Ty, takes a long drag. "I saved someone's life last night."

"What?"

"At the store—some old guy collapsed in front of the entrance. I gave him CPR."

"Jesus. How'd you learn to do that?"

"You know I was a lifeguard."

Ty laughs. "Sorry, I just can't picture you as a lifeguard."

"Oh yeah, even wore the little red speedo."

Ty laughs again. "So what? You're like a hero, right? Are they gonna give you a promotion?"

Bill takes another puff and passes the blunt back. "I got fired."

"Wait—what the fuck?"

"I was smoking weed behind the store with Ryan. The manager smelled it."

"But you saved a guy's life."

"That's what I said. But they brought in the HR manager, some serious-looking soccer mom, who told me I had to take a drug test."

"You said no?"

"I said no."

Ty takes a puff, taps the ashes onto a dirty plate. "I'm proud of you, man. You stood up for yourself."

"But I lost my job."

"We'll figure something out. Kenny called, says he has a big crop coming down next week and he needs help trimming."

"I'm tired of this shit, Ty. We're always chasing the rent, going from shitty job to shitty job. I'm gonna write something—write a book about it."

"That's great. You should write something. You're always saying how you want to write something."

"This isn't the life I want, eating scraps from the corporate table. I need passion! Where's my old typewriter? I need to feel the keys clacking."

"Didn't you sell it for weed money?"

"I'd never sell my typewriter."

"Then it's still under your bed."

He gets up, walks across the living room to the hall closet. "I think I've got some paper in here somewhere."

"I'm having Dylan over tonight."

Bill digs through cardboard boxes and stacks of old, unopened mail. "Aren't you worried?"

"Huh?"

"Worried to bring her back here? This place is a mess—your dirty underwear all over the floor."

"She's cool with my bohemian tendencies."

"Good for you, little bro. But I still think you should clean the place up—maybe just a little."

"Sure thing, man. I'll tidy up when I finish this blunt."

Bill rolls his eyes. "Good luck with that." He takes a can of ginger ale from the fridge and disappears into the bedroom.

Ty swings his legs onto the couch and rests his heavy head on the armrest. He twists the blunt between his fingers and takes a long, thin drag. It's burning down, he thinks. Maybe I should roll another?

43.

Don Ulibarri can't distinguish between the leftover smell of rotting meat and the stench of his own body. Besides losing track of the days, he's also lost a lot of weight—his kidnappers are hardly good providers.

Out in the warehouse, a metal door swings open. There's the sound of footsteps and arguing.

"We're stuck," she says. "We've tried everything. There's no money. The guy's an even bigger loser than we thought."

Then he hears Jackson say, "What about the rings? They're worth at least a hundred grand. He's the fucking quarterback."

"You're so stupid." Her voice is bitter and cracks. "It's all over the news about a famous quarterback missing. You think you're just gonna walk into a pawn shop and sell his Super Bowl rings?"

"There's gotta be someone wants to buy 'em who won't ask questions."

"Yeah—or maybe you go to jail, and I'm not having that. You only play at being a thug. You'll break under the pressure and give me up."

"Fuck you, Vicky. You know, maybe if you didn't do so many drugs and tweak out all of the time—"

"Says the punk with felony charges."

"I'm only in this mess because I said your cocaine was mine. I went to jail for you and this is how you treat me?"

"You weren't complaining when your dick was between my legs!"

Don listens to her yell and cry about money and sex and drugs and how her parents will never forgive her. After a minute she tires out.

Then Jackson says, "We gotta let him go, Vicky."

"We can't. We'll go to prison."

"I'm not gonna kill someone. It's gone too far, Vic. We messed up. We've got to live with that."

"You will kill him," she says. "You're not doing this to me, Jackson. You're not fucking doing this!" She stops herself, regroups. "I love you, baby. It'll all be okay. We'll kill him, dump the body somewhere—be together forever. We'll be together, baby. Finally, just the two of us."

Their voices move closer until the door opens. Don watches them enter the room from his spot on the floor.

Jackson squats down, rips the tape from his mouth. "She wants me to kill you. She thinks we'll go to prison if I don't."

Don's throat is dry. His lips are chapped and sore from the tape. "I won't—I won't say anything. I swear. Don't kill me." He wishes he could fight. His arms, tied behind his back for days, have gone numb.

"See," says Jackson, "he's not gonna tell anyone. It's okay."

Vicky shakes her head in disgust. "You really believe that? God, you're stupid. You're a great fuck, babe, but you're stupid."

"I just wanna forget this," says Don. "Forget you, this place, forget the whole thing ever happened. I just wanna go home."

"Let him go, Vicky."

"Fuck that," she says. "Don't be a pussy. Take that fucking electrical cord and strangle him."

Don thinks maybe he'll die here, covered in his own filth on the floor of an abandoned warehouse. Some end to a brilliant life. The press will cover it, of course. They'll hold memorials and people will talk about him forever. He wonders if his mother, in the long-term care center in Florida, will understand when they give her the news. She's so beautiful, he thinks, and I never noticed. The thought of it makes him sad.

"You're fucking crazy, Vicky. I'm not strangling Don Ulibarri. If you want to kill him you can do it yourself." Jackson turns and walks out of the room.

She screams and storms out behind him.

Don shifts his weight around, tries to get comfortable. He wiggles his arms until he feels warm blood flowing into his bound hands. If you're gonna kill me, he thinks, just fucking do it already.

He tries to sleep. The sound of a mouse scurrying along the floorboard keeps him awake.

44.

Bill stumbles into the living room and finds Ty sprawled out on the couch, another blunt burning down in his hand. "Chicks dig effort," he says. "I'm telling you to tidy up."

"Maybe you're right."

The intercom buzzes.

"Too late," says Bill. "She's here."

"Ah, shit." Ty rushes around the room in a figure-eight, grabbing underwear and crusty socks and tossing them into the bedroom. "What was I thinking?"

"You smoked too much and you weren't thinking."

There's another buzz at the intercom.

Bill laughs. "Do you want to get the door or should I?"

"I'll get it, just don't embarrass me."

"I'd never—"

Ty opens the door and Dylan steps in. She carries a bottle of wine in one hand, puts it on the counter and gives Ty a big kiss, tells him how much she missed him since the last time they hung out.

Ty blushes a little. "Where's your friend? I thought she was coming."

"Oh, she couldn't make it, something about work and getting up early. It's just me. Is that okay?"

"Yeah, that's even better."

They open the wine and drink. Pretty soon they're on the couch, all three of them laughing at YouTube videos on Dylan's phone. Then Dylan says she wants to smoke and Bill says he'll load a bowl.

He smashes a chunky nug into the grinder. "So Dylan, let me get this straight. You don't mind Ty's smelly feet?"

She wrinkles her nose up and makes a silly face. "I kinda think it's cute."

"Good for you, Ty." Bill gives him a hard slap on the knee. "You finally found a chick weird enough to like you."

Ty hides his face in embarrassment and thinks of a way to change the subject. "Bill just saved a guy's life."

Dylan takes the bait. "What happened?"

"Not much," says Bill. "I got fired."

"Fired?"

"Yeah. But it's kind of a long story. Why don't you tell me about the first time you guys met?"

45.

Elmo looks around the crappy motel room, flips through channels on the ancient TV then gives up and goes outside for a cigarette.

He's leaning against the railing, smoking, when a car pulls up to a ground floor room. Deep bass pumps from the trunk. The door opens and a cloud of thick smoke pours out. Kids, wannabe thugs in baggy t-shirts, gather in the parking lot. One of them carries a pack of beer and another is smoking a blunt. Elmo knows he won't get much sleep tonight.

Fuck this, he thinks. He gets his keys and goes for a drive; he always did his best thinking on the road.

He cracks the window of his borrowed car and lights another cigarette, drives through rich and poor neighborhoods and spots a drug house in Globeville. At a four-way stop he makes eye contact with a policeman in a cruiser. He tips his finger to his right eye in salute, the officer gestures back through the windshield as they pass in opposite directions.

He finds a cluster of old warehouses southwest of downtown, parks beneath a high overpass and lights his fifth cigarette since he left the motel. It's time, he thinks, for me to go back to El Paso, to my life of retirement. Let Tony figure this shit out, I'm getting too old.

Then he sees a rusty Subaru, sitting alone in the dark space of an empty warehouse parking lot. "What the fuck?" He squints and tries to read the license plate. "That's it," he says, "447-FRX." He takes a drag of his cigarette to calm his thumping heart. Fuck retirement.

He's about to step out of the car when the side door of the warehouse flings open. A band of yellow light sweeps across the parking lot and two figures move through the open doorway. A man and a woman are arguing.

"You're so stupid," says the woman. "Did you really think we were going to let him go?"

"Yeah, once they paid the money."

"Don't be so naive," she says. "We were always going to kill him."

"You're fucked up. Like, truly fucked in the head."

"That's how it works. You can't have any evidence."

"I wish I never met you."

She stops to say something beneath her breath, slaps him hard across the face.

He winds up like he might hit her back, then turns and walks to the car. In the light of a streetlamp Elmo gets a good look at her face, recognizes the party girl from the Instagram pics.

She's still screaming at the man. "Where do you think you're going?"

"Away from you," he says. "I gotta clear my head."

"This won't go away, not unless you kill him."

He ignores her and climbs into the tiny Subaru; a pair of headlight beams cut through the windshield of Elmo's Cadillac. Soon they're swinging left, and the rusty little car pulls out of the parking lot, spitting gravel from beneath the tires. Elmo watches Vicky go back through the side door and lights another cigarette.

"What?" The voice on the end of the phone sounds sleepy.

"Listen, Eddie. It's me, Elmo."

"It's late, Elmo."

"I found the girl. If we're lucky, I found Ulibarri."

"Huh?"

"Do I have to spell it out for you, Eddie? Just pick up Tony and get down here right away. I'm texting you the address."

It takes him another minute to send the text message. Who made the buttons on these things so damn small? Then he opens the car door, takes another drag, lets his eyes adjust to the darkness as he makes his way across the empty lot. The only sound is the distant passing of cars overhead and the scraping of cowboy boots on dirty asphalt.

Vicky Lipinski is tired of weak men. First, her pathetic father. Now Jackson. When will I meet a man, she thinks, with the balls to do a job?

The door creaks open. "Jackson?" She knew he'd be right back. They always come back.

Silence. Her eyes strain to make out the figure walking towards her.

Scrape. Scrape.

"Jackson?" This time more timid. "Don't fuck with me."

A strange man moves into the light—a wrinkled, scarred face. She screams and tries to run. But he moves quickly for his age, wraps his arms around her from behind. She kicks and bites and flails but the grip around her shoulders is strong.

"Where's Ulibarri?" says the man. "Tell me where he is or I'll kill you."

"He's here," she says. "He's in the other room."

46.

They're halfway through a Seth Rogen movie when there's a rapid buzzing on the intercom. Bill stumbles over and presses the button. "Hello?"

"It's Jackson. Let me in." His voice is shaky, worked-up.

Bill presses another button and a moment later there's a loud knock. Jackson steps inside, paces back and forth across the living room.

Ty speaks in his cheerful tone. "Where you been? This is my friend Dylan, I don't think you've met."

She tries to wave hello, notices the plastic bracelet on his ankle and wonders what he did to end up wearing it.

But Jackson doesn't stop for introductions. "It's Vicky," he says, still pacing. "We're in so much trouble."

"Calm down." Bill wonders if Jackson is high on something. "Sounds like you're not having a good night. Why don't we go into the other room and leave these kids out here to have fun?" He pulls at Jackson's arm, leads him into the bedroom and they both sit down on the edge of the bed. "Tell me what happened?"

Jackson drops his shoulders forward, hangs his head. "Vicky and I had a big fight. I took her car and drove away."

"I thought you weren't going to see her anymore. Isn't she the reason you're wearing that ridiculous Orwellian ankle bracelet?"

"Orwellian?" He looks confused. "It's not that simple. I'm in love with her, bro. But we did something really stupid."

"Tell me she's not pregnant."

"Fuck, man. No, she's not pregnant. But we did something really bad, Bill. Something against the law. And now there's no way out."

"I don't understand. What did you do?"

"You know that quarterback? Don Ulibarri?"

"I heard on the news he went missing. The cops are turning the city upside down looking for him."

"They won't find him."

"Jackson, tell me you didn't—"

"We kidnapped him. I knocked him out with a baseball bat and Vicky backed her car up to his garage."

Bill tries to imagine Jackson swinging a bat at the quarterback. It's too ridiculous, even for him. "Oh fuck, Jackson. What the fuck did you do?"

"It was Vicky's idea—we had it all planned out. We'd kidnap the guy and hide him in a warehouse, collect some ransom money. He's a famous quarterback, has all those car dealerships. We figured some-one's gotta pay up."

"You didn't kill him, did you?"

"No, but Vicky wants me to do it." Jackson buries his face in his hands. "He's still at the warehouse, chained to a steel pole. The fucker is dead broke."

"Don Ulibarri is chained up in a warehouse? And broke?" Bill's vision goes a little blurry and he rolls back onto the mattress. "Jackson, you're so fucked."

"I know, man." Jackson sobs, mushy tears wetting his face. "I know."

"I'm in." Ty imagines himself rescuing Don Ulibarri and getting interviewed on the evening news.

Dylan crosses her arms. "You can't be serious?"

"Jackson's my friend." He takes one last hit, pulls on his shoes. "He needs my help."

"You think you can just untie a football legend, dust him off and say sorry and everything will be okay?"

Jackson is still sobbing. Bill shrugs. "If you've got a better idea let's hear it."

She turns back to Ty. "Don't do this."

"I always help my friends."

"Even when your friends are violent criminals? We should call the police."

He looks down at the floor and ties his shoelaces, doesn't answer.

She sighs. "It's been great, Ty. I'm going home."

"Dylan, wait—"

The door closes and she's gone.

47.

He binds Vicky's hands behind her with duct tape. Then he goes to the car and comes back with two heavy jumper cables, uses them to tie her upright to a support column.

"Who are you?" The words come out shaky. She regroups and puts on her best attempt at a tough face.

He doesn't answer.

"What do you want?"

Silence.

"I told you, Ulibarri's in the other room."

He smiles. "Yes, but I'm also here for you."

She twists her body violently and screams, the sound bouncing through the rafters of the building and then disappearing into the darkness.

Elmo chuckles and lights a cigarette. "Ain't nobody gonna hear you."

But she screams and screams, until Elmo takes a red bandana from his pocket and ties it around her mouth. "I'm gonna have fun with you."

The sound of tires rolling over gravel drifts in from the parking lot. He's expecting Tony and Eddie, but Elmo doesn't like to take chances. He leaves her in the center of the room and hides in a shadow.

The door opens. "Vicky? You still here?"

Elmo recognizes the voice as the man she was arguing with earlier, waits for him to come through the door to catch him by surprise.

"Vicky? Hello?" Jackson steps into the dark space.

Elmo is quick to get an arm around his shoulders, the other brings a knife up to his throat. "Got you now, little fucker!" He's so excited to make his catch that he hardly notices Bill and Ty rushing him from the doorway. He pulls the knife from Jackson's throat and slashes forward just in time to catch the edge of Ty's hand with the blade.

Ty jumps back in surprise and grabs his cut hand. Blood runs between his fingers and onto the floor.

Bill is frozen. He tries to think of something, to turn and run, but it's already too late. A pair of fat men—one of them waving a gun around—slide in from the parking lot, grab him by the shirt with pudgy hands.

Tony laughs. "Some party you've got here, Elmo. Looks like you could really use the help."

Elmo wipes the sweat from his forehead. "I had it under control."

"Sure." Tony turns to bark at Eddie. "Find some more tape. Get 'em tied up."

Eddie snaps to action and Elmo lights another cigarette.

"I keep telling you to get a pistol." Tony flashes the weighty handgun around in the dim light, finger still on the trigger. "They're useful in such moments."

Elmo takes a long drag and shrugs.

"Don here?"

He motions over his shoulder. "In the back."

Tony pulls a cigar from his shirt pocket, rolls it around in his mouth. "You're worth the price, Elmo. God bless Texas."

48.

Oscar Martinez sits alone in his office. He sips from a glass of whiskey and rolls a small joint, twists the end up and lights it with a gag-pistol lighter. He imagines that silly look Ty gets on his face after a few too many hits. Damn, he thinks, it's just not the same without him.

It's not like he doesn't understand what the kid is going through. It's a tough business. Sometimes the ones you like are the ones you have to send to jail.

But I'm just another immigrant, he thinks. I didn't make the rules. I earn my money, feed my family, live another day. And then this kid, some stupid long-haired hippy, makes me feel guilty about it.

He sits in the quiet office for a long time; doesn't move from the chair. The cannabinoids take effect. He traces his finger along the edge of the whiskey glass and speaks to an empty room. "I gotta make this right."

He sends a text: "Where are you? Let's talk."

The joint burns down to a tiny roach and he waits.

But there's no reply.

49.

They're marched in a line down a narrow hall—Vicky, too—into one of the dark, wood-paneled offices at the back of the warehouse.

"Stick out your hands," says Eddie.

Ty does what he's told. They're wrapping duct tape around his wrists when he feels the phone, still hidden in his pocket, start to vibrate. He works to keep a straight face, hopes the hairy man doesn't notice.

"Hey, what's that?"

Too late. "What's what?"

"That vibrating noise." Eddie reaches a bandaged hand into Ty's skinny jeans, finds the phone.

"For fuck's sake, Eddie." Tony is still waving the gun around, a cigar in the other hand. "You were supposed to search them for that kind of shit."

"I'm sorry, boss."

"Don't tell me you're sorry, Eddie. Do you know what happens when a hostage has a cell phone?" He tucks the pistol back into his waistband. "They call the fucking police, you moron."

"Geez, Tony. I'm sorry. I don't know what else to tell you."

"Please," says Bill, "my friend is hurt real bad. He needs medical attention."

"You mean that little cut?" Tony grins over his shoulder at Elmo. "That ain't so bad."

"Just let me take him for help." Bill pleads. "We won't say anything."

"You think I'm some kind of idiot? What's it gonna matter when you're dead?"

"You won't kill us."

"Oh, yeah?" Tony seems amused. "How are you so sure?"

"Because you're businessmen, not murderers."

"Let me tell you something." Tony puffs up his chest. "Back in El Paso, me and Elmo here had a nice little side hustle running wetbacks across the border."

"Tony—" Elmo interrupts.

"Who's he gonna tell? Ain't no harm in saying. Anyway, one day our driver shows up with a box truck full of dead Mexicans. Guess it got too hot back there or he forgot to give them water or something. So we kill the driver and light the whole mess of them on fire, even the truck, way out in the desert." He pauses for effect. "Can't have no loose ends."

Elmo winces. "Tony—"

Tony spins around on his heels. "What?"

"Stop talking."

"They ain't gonna say nothing." He chuckles. "They'll be dead soon."

Elmo scratches his forehead. "That's a lot of killing."

"Yeah? So then what am I paying you for?"

Elmo lights another cigarette, stalls for a moment. "You pay me to be smart, and I think we should talk to Ulibarri—get the whole story before we go making any quick decisions."

Tony scoffs. "You were never any fucking fun."

They're left alone in the dark room, wedged shoulder to shoulder between a rusty metal desk and a turned-over filing cabinet. Blood oozes down the silver tape around Ty's hands and collects in a little pool on the concrete.

"Keep them up," says Bill, "to stop the bleeding." With his own bound hands he tears a strip from the bottom of his shirt, ties it tightly around Ty's wound. "You'll be okay. It looks worse than it is."

Ty smiles.

"Let's be quiet, see if we can hear something useful."

"Bill—"

"Yeah?"

"I have to pee."

There's a buzz in Eddie's pocket—the phone he confiscated from the skinny kid.

A text reads: "Where are you? Let's talk."

Eddie holds the phone up. "It's from Oscar. Who do you think that is?"

"Who cares?" Tony snickers as he lights another cigar. "He ain't nothin to me."

50.

The whiskey isn't helping; Oscar still feels bad about their argument. The joint isn't doing much either—every skunky hit reminds him of Ty.

He looks at his phone again. No returned text. No voicemail. "Damn it, kid. Now I'm getting worried."

He taps an icon on the screen. An app loads. There's a map with a little blinking dot—Ty's location. Not exactly a good place to be, he thinks. Especially this late at night.

He grabs his scratched-up revolver from the desk drawer, the car keys from a hook by the back door. The old Buick's parked in the alley behind the dumpster—same place he always leaves her.

51.

Tony kicks him a few times. "Get up you old sack of shit. It's Tony."

Fuck, he thinks, how did he find me here? He groans, struggles to sit up straight against the wall.

"It's been a while, Ulibarri. You're hard to find." Tony leans in real close, rips the tape from Don's mouth.

"Been right here." He coughs—a dry, dusty rattle.

"How convenient."

Don looks around the room, nods at the chain around his ankles and the shit bucket in the corner. "I'd say otherwise."

"Is this some kind of joke? You planning to bounce to Mexico and disappear with my money?"

"Jesus, Tony! Look at my fucking face. Does it look like I'm going to Mexico?"

Tony's quiet for a minute, thinking. Then he rocks back and laughs. "You know what the funny part is? They actually thought you had money. Well now that we're all here—"

"For fuck's sake, Tony. Get me out of these chains."

"—I have some questions I've been dying to ask you. Let's start with, where the fuck is my quarter million?"

"There was a problem across the border."

"What problem?"

"My guy—" Don coughs again. "He's dead."

"What the fuck do you mean your guy is dead?"

"He's fucking dead, Tony. Things are crazy as shit down there."

"So where's the coke?"

"Still in Mexico."

"Can you get it?"

"Tony, I don't think you understand—they cut his fucking head off."

"So get a new guy. What's the problem?"

"It's gone, Tony. The coke is gone." He remembers his first Super Bowl, the feeling that he'd live forever. Now he's on the floor of a leaky warehouse, his back all fucked up from sleeping on concrete. And the only guy who comes looking for him is Tony Giannopoulos. His eyes get wet.

"You know, before I knew the real Don Ulibarri, I actually looked up to you—thought you were some kind of hero." Tony looks right into Don's teary eyes. "I'm sorry, Don. This is gonna hurt."

52.

The old Buick slows to an easy stop. The warehouse is off in the distance; a single streetlight illuminates a corner of the dark parking lot. Oscar scans the building with a pair of binoculars. Two cars are parked along the north side, an old Subaru and a silver Cadillac. He scribbles the license plate numbers on a sticky note and calls a friend. "Ronnie, how you been?"

Ronnie sounds tired on the other end. "Why the fuck are you calling me so late?"

"You're at work, right?"

"I was taking a nap."

"In your patrol car?"

"Where else?"

"Denver's finest—"

"Shut the fuck up."

"Listen, Ronnie. I need you to do me a professional favor—got a couple of plates for you to run."

"Sure thing, Oscar. Text me that shit. Hey, when do you need it?"

"Now."

"Why? What are you up to?"

"Just run the plates, Ronnie. Call me when it's done."

"Oscar—"

"Just do it, Ronnie." He hangs up. His eyes adjust to the night as he settles in, sips cold coffee and waits like he's done a thousand times before.

Fuck, he thinks, now I've got to pee. He opens the door and swings his legs out, pisses on the asphalt between his boots. Then he slides back into the seat, lights a cigarette and tries to relax. He doesn't have to wait long.

He takes another sip of cold coffee. "Missing?"

"Yep, reported missing by the parents just yesterday." Ronnie says it matter-of-factly. "And get this, a month or so back she gets busted with some guy for snorting blow and driving drunk on Lincoln. Holy shit, this girl's mug shot is fucking hot. Serious masturbation material."

"Jesus, Ronnie. What about the other car?"

"Hold on, give me a second."

Oscar can hear him on the other end of the line, typing on his in-car laptop.

When he comes back his voice is sober. "Oscar, where the fuck are you?"

"Why?"

"Just tell me, Oscar."

"Some old warehouse under the Colfax overpass, near the football stadium."

"What's the address? Text it to me now."

"Okay, okay."

"You're sure about the license plate on the Cadillac?"

"I'm looking at it now."

"Don't move," says Ronnie. "And don't do anything stupid. Just send me the fucking address."

"What's going on?"

"The car belongs to Tony Giannopoulos."

"Giannopoulos?"

"Runs payday loan shops all over town."

"What's the problem?"

"Money laundering, drug deals, prostitution, fake immigration documents—you name it, Giannopoulos is deep into it. We've been trying to pin a case on him for years, never can get a witness to testify."

"Fuck."

"Fuck is right. Now you just sit tight, buddy. Denver Police are on the way."

Yeah, Oscar thinks, that's what I'm afraid of. His hand fumbles through the trash on the passenger seat. Where the fuck are my cigarettes?

53.

When Don Ulibarri first came to find himself on the floor of this dingy little prison, chained like a fucking animal, he was sure a few ribs were bruised. The punk might be stupid, but he knows how to swing a baseball bat.

Now, after the beating Tony gave him, it feels like every bone in his body is cracked and broken. His cheeks bleed, smashed against his teeth. A gash across his forehead drips blood into his eyes and mouth. His stomach is stiff and bruised, and he wonders if he's not bleeding to death on the inside.

He was surprised to see Tony. At least here, in this godforsaken place, he had imagined he was free of Tony's reach. But bad money never goes away.

It's funny, he thinks, I'd give anything just to see my mom. I guess we always want our moms in the end.

He laughs a little and the motion sends a stabbing pain through his gut. He tastes blood, can't see, can't lift his hands to wipe his eyes.

"Fuck," he says out loud to the shitty room. "What a stupid place to die."

He plays with the heavy rings on his fingers, spins them around. Where are the reporters now? The fans? It's all for nothing, all for fucking nothing.

Then an anger flares inside of him. First a burning in his chest then a fire behind his eyes. I'm Don Ulibarri. I won two Super Bowls. "Fuck this. I'm going home."

He twists, thumps against the ground with all of his energy and manages to slide onto his stomach. Thick bands of heavily-wrapped duct tape still bind his wrists behind his back. He pulls his fists apart, manages to force open a tiny gap and work the chain from his ankles into the space. His back strains. He kicks and the chain cuts into the tape. He rocks forwards and resets the chain. Kicks again. And again.

Metal burns his wrists. He breaths and grunts. Back and forth. Each kick bringing him closer to freedom.

He's exhausted. He rests and listens in the dark. Doors open and close across the hall. Footsteps echo in the warehouse.

Then he kicks again. And again.

Exhaustion. Rest again.

Then kick.

Then rest.

He struggles to breath through chapped lips. The room spins. He lays very still and doesn't move.

He thinks of the shitty car dealerships, of a failed marriage and the sad excuse for a person he's become. And the fire comes back. The anger. The fucking rage.

And he kicks again. Takes a deep breath. Kicks again. Breathes. Kicks again.

The tape rips. His arms spread out flat beside him on the floor and his lungs pump hard. Thank God, he thinks, thank God.

His energy is nearly gone; the anger won't sustain him forever. I have one chance to put up my fight. One last chance or I'm dead, and I don't want to die today.

54.

Tony paces like he always does when he's worked up. Elmo is smoking a cigarette, lights one for Tony. "Fuck, man. What a waste of time this has all been."

"Time?" Tony takes the cigarette and pulls a long, smooth drag. "You're worried about time? I'm the one out two hundred and fifty large plus whatever I shelled out to drag you up from Texas. No money, and no fucking cocaine!"

"The guy's so fucking poor the IRS ain't even collecting."

"Now you're funny?"

"Relax, Tony. There's nothing we can do. Let's go out for a big meal and you can drink until you pass out. Maybe even get a hooker."

"I got a better idea."

"Yeah?"

"I'm gonna kill that worthless fucker, put a bullet into his thick forehead and watch it split open."

"You don't wanna do that."

"What makes you think I don't want to shoot the bastard?"

"I know you wanna shoot the bastard, but it's not a smart idea." He stamps out his cigarette butt and lights a new one. "It's just that it's gonna take a lot of work to move him, clean up the mess, get rid of the body."

"That's what I got Eddie for."

"It's not like that, Tony. All these witnesses, it's gonna be a real problem."

"What fucking witnesses? A few stupid kids? I'm killing that bastard even if I have to wrap my hands around his thick neck and choke him."

Eddie, listening to their conversation from a distance, finally works up the courage to speak. "Elmo's right. If you kill Ulibarri, you gotta kill 'em all, and I didn't sign up to kill no college kids."

Tony's face goes red. "You'll do whatever I fucking tell you to do. If your wife wasn't my sister I'd throw you out on the street."

"Just think about it, Tony. You shoot those kids it's gonna be a lot of noise, a lot of work getting the bodies out. Someone's gonna hear something, see something, call the cops."

"Fuck the kids. We'll move Ulibarri and I'll do him someplace else."

Elmo steps in between them, shakes his head. "They saw our faces, heard our names. If Ulibarri disappears they'll send the cops right after us. We're fucked, Tony. Totally fucked."

Tony still paces in a tight pattern, leather soles grinding on the turn. "Then what do we do?"

"We cut him free," says Elmo. "Drop his ass off at a local emergency room. Ain't getting the money back either way."

"And the bastard gets a free pass?" He stops pacing.

"Ulibarri walks, Tony. It's the only way. The motherfucker is gonna be so happy just to live, he ain't gonna say shit. Same goes for the girl and her dumbass boyfriend. We explain things to the others—it was all just a misunderstanding, a case of mistaken identity."

"Damn it," says Tony. "You're fucking right and I hate it."

"That's why you hire me." Elmo works at the stiffness in his neck, rubs a sore spot with his rough fingertips. "I gotta get some air, figure out how to make this all happen." He swivels on his cowboy boots and walks to the rear emergency door, pushes it open by the long, rusty handle.

"Don't go far," says Tony. "Eddie ain't much company."

But he's already gone.

Tony stares at Eddie, doesn't say anything.

"What? My fucking fly open?"

"How about I shoot you instead?"

"Huh?"

"Think about it. You're my brother-in-law. I got a half a million dollar life insurance policy on your chubby ass."

"Tony—"

"Half a million is just about enough to cover this mess." He laughs. "I could even take a vacation, maybe take the wife back to Italy. She's always begging, and the Amalfi Coast is gorgeous in summer—water so fucking blue."

Eddie is trembling. He looks down at the bandages on his hand, then back at Tony. "You're kidding, right? You would never do that."

Tony replies with a blank stare. Tears build in Eddie's soft eyes.

"Shh," says Tony. "Did you hear that?"

"Hear what?"

"Listen."

A soft mumble comes from the other room.

"I told those fucking kids to stay quiet." He pulls the gun from his waistband, waves it around over his head. "Little bastards."

"Calm down, boss."

"Those kids think they can fuck with me—they don't even know who I am, what I do to people. You all think you can fuck with me!"

"No, Tony—"

"And that motherfucker Elmo! He thinks he can fuck with me, too. Takes my money and tells me to let Don Ulibarri walk away. I've had it with all of you!"

He marches down the hall to the little office, kicks open the door and grabs Bill by the hair. Vicky Lipinski screams. He drags Bill out into the open warehouse, tells Eddie to get the rest of them.

"But, Tony—"

"Do as I fucking say! Or I'll shoot you with 'em."

They're assembled together on the concrete floor and Tony puts the gun to Bill's head. "You know who I am, little punk? I'm Tony Giannopoulos. That's who. Remember that for the last ten seconds of your life."

He pushes Bill down to the floor, goes to pull the trigger.

Ty screams. "Wait!"

One last thought passes through Bill's head, a memory of summer camp. He was thirteen, tiptoeing from the cabin after lights out to meet Connie Bodzewski behind the archery shed.

There's an ear-splitting crash and he jerks to the side. Am I dead?

He opens his eyes in time to see the armored policemen streaming single-file through the door, each one breaking off into a different direction.

"DROP THE WEAPON!" They shout over each other. "DROP THE WEAPON OR I'LL FUCKING KILL YOU!"

Tony drops the gun to the floor and a pair of masked officers wrestle him to the ground. Eddie goes peacefully, spreads out flat as a knee drives into his back and his arms are jerked up behind him.

"Hey," says one of the officers, "this one pissed himself."

And all the masked faces have a laugh.

55.

Don Ulibarri strains to hear the commotion. There's a loud crash in the warehouse, the sound of footsteps and shouting. His mind races and his thoughts become jumbled and twisted. The days and nights all passing in the same room have gone to his head.

It'll feel good to fight, he thinks. It's been a long time since I've fought.

Then the door splinters at the lock and hinges. A dark figure rushes in.

Don lunges forward in one gigantic motion, throws every remaining scrap of energy into his assault.

He doesn't see the bullet that drops him. There's only a loud pop, the room spinning and turning black, and the roaring—pulsing—of a cheering crowd.

"Holy fucking shit!" Ronnie pulls the mask off his face, works to catch his breath. "I shot him! I fucking shot him!"

Another officer speaks into a radio, "Shots fired. Suspect down.

I repeat, shots fired. One suspect down." He looks at Ronnie. "You okay?"

"Am I okay? I'm better than okay. I'm fucking great!"

"Focus," says the officer. "He came at you. He tried to grab your gun."

"Right," says Ronnie. "He tried to grab my gun."

"It was the only thing you could do. Now help me give CPR."

They get down on the ground, hear officers across the hall shouting back and forth as they clear each room. Ronnie's partner leans over the bloody and beaten face, listens for a breath. "Holy shit."

"What?"

"It's Don Ulibarri."

"No fucking way. The quarterback?"

"It's him! Look at those rings!"

Ronnie looks at the man's hand, pieces of duct tape still plastered to the wrist. A pair of gold Super Bowl rings glisten under a layer of dirt and dried blood. "I can't believe it," he says. "I idolized that guy."

"Dude," says the faceless partner, "you're gonna have so much paperwork."

56.

Elmo's across the street, smoking in a dark shadow, when the police vans pull up outside the warehouse. He drops his cigarette to the ground, taps it out gently with the tip of his boot and walks away in silence. He never bothers looking back.

He catches a cab six blocks away. "Take me to the El Limousine station, I'm late for my bus."

He's a few hours south of the city, watching the pine trees and wild grass give way to sagebrush and tumbleweed, when he lets out a little laugh and eases back into the dirty seat. In an hour the sun will rise.

The woman in the next seat hears his chuckle, turns and introduces herself in the quiet space of the dark bus. "Are you going to El Paso for business?"

He thinks for a minute, laughs again. "No, no," he says. "I'm retired."

57.

A paramedic brings them blankets, a second one bandages Ty's hand. The night air isn't cold but it seems natural to huddle together under the scratchy brown wool like victims on the evening news. A helicopter circles overhead and more officials arrive on the scene. Camera crews mingle together, people drinking coffee from styrofoam cups.

Ty spots Oscar across the crowd, drops his blanket and waves his arms over his head. It takes Oscar another minute to cross the police barricade, past technicians and investigators and photographers. He wears his bail enforcement badge on a chain outside his shirt. "Fucking circus," he says. "You okay, kid?"

"A little cut up but we're alright."

"What happened?"

Ty rubs his forehead. "Jackson kidnapped Don Ulibarri."

"The quarterback?"

"Yeah, the fucking quarterback. He's dead. Cops shot him."

Oscar goes to light a cigarette and one of the crime scene technicians barks at him. "Your friend Jackson, is he dead?"

"Nah, the cops hauled him off with his girlfriend. Oh, and a couple of loan sharks."

"Tony Giannopoulos?"

Ty nods. "And some guy named Eddie."

"Dangerous people, kid. You're lucky to be alive."

"I'm glad to see you."

"Glad to see you too, kid. I'm sorry I got so upset."

Ty lowers his head. "It's my fault. I quit the business."

"Nah, kid. You're too good for this shit. Come on, I'll take you to the emergency room. My cousin's wife is a nurse at Denver Health." He slaps one of the paramedics on the shoulder. "Ain't no use paying these guys a thousand bucks for a ride up the road."

"Oscar, how many cousins do you have?"

"I don't know," he says. "I lost count."

They're halfway across the parking lot when Ronnie breaks away from another officer and comes jogging over. "Oscar!"

"Damn, Ronnie. You weren't fucking around."

Ronnie leans forward, makes a face like he's sharing a bit of gossip. "I finally got to use my gun—the fucking carbine. One shot." He flexes his chest and shoulders, brings his hands together over his belt buckle. "Right in the face."

"Jesus."

"You'll never believe it—it was Ulibarri, Don Ulibarri. Fucker went down hard."

Oscar looks around. "The media is everywhere, Ronnie—maybe you could show some remorse."

"Fuck 'em! Captain says it was a clean shot. They're sending a union rep down to handle the paperwork." He rocks back on his heels. "I'm gonna be okay."

"That's good, Ronnie. Real good."

"Hey, you gonna be at poker this week?"

"I think I'm gonna skip it—lot of shit to catch up on."

"I hear you, buddy." Ronnie makes a little shooting motion with his index finger, drops his thumb like the hammer. "See you next time."

"Right," says Oscar, "next time."

He turns the ignition and the old Buick starts up. The radio comes on and he asks what station they like.

Ty reaches up from the backseat and turns the dial. Old-school Chili Peppers plays over shitty speakers and he feels himself relax for the first time all night.

Oscar tells Bill to open the glove box, dig around for a joint in a clear plastic doob tube. Bill rummages around until he finds it, presses the cigarette lighter in and waits for the click. The car fills with smoke.

Ty rolls down his window. "How'd you know where I was?"

"The phone, kid. I installed a tracking app before I gave it to you."

"I guess you'll be wanting that back now."

"You keep it a while—until you find the next thing."

"What next thing?"

"I don't know. That's for you to decide."

"Thanks, Oscar."

"Call me once in awhile, kid. Come by the office and burn a bowl."

"I'd love that."

"Who knows? Maybe you could come along on a pickup for old time's sake. I could always use a good pair of hands."

Ty smiles. "Never say never."

"In that case, I've got this bail skipper, a real problem child. I think he's at the girlfriend's place in Westminster."

"Oscar—"

"Okay, okay. I'm just saying."

"I love you, Oscar. I'll never forget what you did for me."

Oscar's dark, worn cheeks blush. "I love you too, kid."

58.

Bill and Ty shuffle their feet along the sidewalk. Cars rush by on 13th, people on their way to work or school or someplace important. It's a clear morning; Ty holds his still-bandaged hand up to block the sun from his eyes. "Crazy couple of days, huh?"

"Days? More like weeks."

"You think Dylan will ever talk to me again?"

"Yeah, man. She'll call. You were only trying to help a friend."

"Some friend—he almost got us all killed. She was right, you know. We never should have left the apartment."

Bill laughs. "You always said you wanted adventure."

"Yeah, like rock-climbing or backpacking through South America." He tries to hold back a laugh but can't help himself. "Not armed criminals."

"I guess we don't always choose these things." Bill contemplates their luck for a minute. "So what's next?"

"We've got an eighth of weed and about twenty bucks between us, so I'm thinking we start with breakfast."

Bill smiles. "I know a great little place a few blocks up."

They turn and head up the alley. Bill kicks a rusty can as they walk. There's a man poking through a dumpster with a stick, digging for treasure in a heap of garbage. He stops to watch them pass.

They find Joe tucked into an empty doorway on Colfax. "You guys come for some pills?"

"No thanks, man." Ty laughs and pats him on the shoulder. "But we'll buy you a breakfast burrito."

Joe shakes his head. "I'm gonna stay here and work my corner."

"You sure? Come on back to our place and smoke some tree."

"I've got Percocet. Percocet sells."

"Well if you ever need anything, you let us know."

"I'm fine," says Joe. "I'm always fine."

They start to walk away and Ty stops, turns back. "Does it ever get too hard?"

"What do you mean?"

"I mean your life. It can't be easy."

"You're right. It ain't easy. But one life is as good as another." He holds up a little bag of pills, the end twisted and tied into a knot. "This is my life. This is what I've got."

***

Author's Note

Independent authors thrive only because of readers like you. If you enjoyed this book, please consider leaving a review. It's the best way to continue supporting my work.